Just then, there was a shout and looking up, they saw that the door at the top of the stairs had opened and a guard had emerged, followed by another and another.

'I think that settles it,' Otto said. He stepped onto the carpet, followed quickly by his mother and Cornelius.

There was no doubt that they had come into contact with powerful magic of some kind. Otto could feel a low vibration that seemed to enter his body and make it tingle all over. But the carpet did not move an inch.

'Someone needs to work out how to make this thing fly,' Cornelius said, 'and they need to do it fast!'

ORCHARD BOOKS
338 Euston Road, London NW1 3BH
Orchard Books Australia
Level 17/207 Kent Street, Sydney, NSW 2000

First published in 2011 by Orchard Books

A Paperback Original

ISBN 978 1 40830 681 9

Text © Brian Keaney 2011

A CIP catalogue record for this book is available from the
British Library.

1 3 5 7 9 10 8 6 4 2

Printed in Great Britain

Orchard Books is a division of Hachette Children's Books,
an Hachette UK company.

www.hachette.co.uk

THE MAGICAL DETECTIVES

BRIAN KEANEY

ORCHARD BOOKS

CONTENTS

1

MRS SPINOZA'S WORST FEAR

To look at, there was nothing very remarkable about Otto Spinoza. He was about average height for a boy of twelve. He had very clear blue eyes and floppy brown hair, which he was in the habit of tossing back from his forehead from time to time. His teacher at school thought he was rather quiet, but she concluded that he was merely thoughtful and left it at that.

However, there were at least two things about Otto that *were* very much out of the ordinary. The first was the fact that from as far back as he could remember, Otto had had the feeling that he was different from the other boys and girls in his school; for some reason, which he could not quite put his finger on, he simply did not belong. He didn't talk about this feeling to anyone, because he didn't want to seem rude or stuck-up. But it was always there.

The second unusual thing about Otto was the mystery of his father's death: he had died of a rare tropical disease shortly after Otto was born. So rare was this disease, that no one else in England had ever contracted it, and by the time the hospital realised what was wrong, it was too late to do anything about it. The doctors had been extremely puzzled because even in the jungles of Borneo, where the disease originated, it had only reared its ugly head a few times in the last hundred years. The conclusion they had come to was that Mr Spinoza, who was a bookseller by trade, must have been bitten by an insect that had stowed away in a crate of books he had bought at an auction the week before.

Otto had often wondered why the insect had not bitten anyone else, such as the person who put the books in the crate in the first place, or the auctioneer, but no one seemed to know the answer to this.

Otto and his mother lived in the sleepy little town of Bridlington Chawley, in an apartment above the second-hand bookshop that his mother now ran. It was not the sort of home you see featured in magazines or on television programmes. The furniture was rickety, the carpets threadbare and the rooms all needed a coat of paint. But Otto did not mind all that. He liked living above a bookshop because he loved to read, and there were always plenty of books waiting for his attention.

Otto's mother was a dreadful worrier. When it rained, she worried that the roof might leak, when it was cold she worried that the central heating might break, and when it was warm she worried that it would not last. She worried about her health, and about her weight, about whether or not she was going to be able to pay all the bills. But most of all she worried about Otto, and in particular about what would become of him if anything should happen to her.

'They'll come round sticking their noses in, asking all sorts of questions, that's what they'll do,' she frequently complained. 'Then they'll take you away and put you in a home for orphans. There'll be no one to care for you, no one to look after you. Oh, Otto, I can't bear to think about it!'

At this point she always burst into tears and Otto was obliged to make her a cup of strong tea, and open a packet of biscuits.

Otto's mother had a great fondness for biscuits. They were the only thing that really stopped her worrying for any length of time. It was because of this that Otto was not present when one of the most extraordinary things in the history of Bridlington Chawley took place. She had sent him to the corner shop for a couple of packets of chocolate digestives. So he only discovered what had happened when he returned.

It was the first day of the summer holidays, and all the way to the shop Otto was thinking about what he would do in the weeks to come. Other children in his class went on holiday to exotic places, but there was no chance of that for Otto. Even if they could afford to go away, his mother would be far too worried to contemplate such a trip. Perhaps if his father had been alive, Otto thought to himself, things might have been different.

He was still thinking about what might have been when he arrived back home to find the door of the bookshop wide open and no sign of his mother. Surprised, he stepped into the shop. Immediately the hairs on the back of his neck stood on end and goosebumps sprang up all over his body. The air in the shop seemed to crackle with energy as though a thunderstorm might break out above the bookshelves at any moment. It made Otto quite dizzy. He took hold of a bookcase and steadied himself.

'Mum?' he called out. 'Where are you?'

There was no answer. He walked across the shop and opened the door to the stock room. But it was empty, except for the hundreds and hundreds of characters who lived within the dusty covers of the books. He could almost hear them muttering unhappily to each other, as if they, too, sensed that something was wrong.

Otto looked in the back yard in case his mother was putting out the rubbish. Then he went upstairs and checked the apartment that they both shared. There was no sign of her. But in the kitchen, stuck to the front of the refrigerator door was a set of magnetic letters that had been there ever since he was a baby. He hadn't played with them for many years. They had been rearranged into two words.

HELP ME.

Was this a message from his mother?

Perhaps if you had been in Otto's position,

you would have seriously considered calling the police at this point. But such a thought did not even enter Otto's head. He knew only too well what his mother would think of such behaviour. He could almost hear her voice warning him: They'll put you in a home, Otto.

So what was he to do? *Stay calm, Otto*, he told himself. *Think!*

But it wasn't easy to stay calm. Panic was knocking at the door of his imagination, demanding to be let in. Otto paced about the kitchen trying to make up his mind what to do next. Finally he decided to search the apartment thoroughly. There might be something that would give him a clue as to where his mother had gone. He went into his mother's bedroom and looked in the wardrobe. As far as he could tell, all her clothes were still there.

Then he noticed her diary on the dressing table. He hesitated. His mother was a very private person. Every night without fail she recorded her thoughts in her diary before going to sleep, and never breathed a word about its contents to Otto.

But the time for privacy was past. This was a genuine emergency and Otto simply didn't know what else to do. He sat on the corner of the bed, opened the diary at the first page and began to read. To his disappointment the diary turned out to be astonishingly dull. Despite the great secrecy that surrounded it, there was absolutely nothing important in those pages. His mother wrote about the weather, noted down appointments for the dentist and recorded birds she had seen from her bedroom window. But there was nothing that might give him a clue to where she had gone. With a sigh, Otto closed the diary and put it back on the dressing table.

He was just about to leave the room when he suddenly saw his mother's face in the mirror. She was looking out at him with her familiar worried expression. Otto whirled round, ready to ask her where on earth she had been. But she wasn't there! And when he turned back to the mirror her reflection had vanished.

Had he imagined it? Or had it been real?

He was still trying to make up his mind about this when he heard the doorbell ring. Thinking it must be his mother, he raced downstairs. But to his great disappointment, it turned out to be a man with a shiny bald head and a thick beard with no moustache, so that he looked a bit like his head was upside down. He was carrying a cardboard box full of books that, no doubt, he wanted to sell.

The man could see Otto through the window, so there was nothing to be done but open the door.

'Is the manager available?' the man demanded.

Trying to remain calm, Otto politely explained that the shop was closed because his mother had gone out on an errand.

'And when will she be back?' the man asked, rather irritably.

'Oh, later on some time,' Otto said with a shrug.

Reluctantly, the man turned away and Otto was just about to shut the door when he saw a tall girl with bobbed hair and glasses, striding purposefully towards him. His heart sank. It was Juliet Pennington. She was in his class at school and she was not the kind of person to take no for an answer.

'Hello, Otto,' she said, marching straight into the shop before he had a chance to tell her that it was closed. 'Have you got any books about Roman coins?'

'I don't know,' Otto said. He was flustered

now. If he told her his mother had popped out on an errand Juliet would probably decide to wait until she came back. With a sigh, he decided that the easiest way to get rid of her was to serve her himself. It wouldn't be difficult. The prices of the books were written on the inside covers in pencil and he knew how the till worked.

'There are some books about Ancient Rome over there,' Otto told her, pointing to the history section. 'I don't know whether there's anything about coins.'

'And do you have any books on training cats?'

Training cats! Otto shook his head. He had always thought there was something a bit odd about Juliet. 'I don't think it's possible to train cats,' he told her.

'It must be,' she replied.

Remembering what his mother often said – that the customer was always right – Otto showed her where the books on animals were shelved. Then he sat behind the counter, trying to look as if everything was perfectly normal.

She seemed to spend ages looking at the books, but at last she came up to the counter with a couple of books and the correct money ready in her hand. 'How come you're running the shop today?' she asked.

Otto mumbled something about his mother going to a book-buying conference, but he felt himself blushing as he did so. He had never been any good at lying.

As soon as she leaves the shop, I'm going to turn the sign in the window to 'closed' and lock the door, Otto told himself. And I'm not answering it to anyone else, unless it's my mum.

But as Juliet turned from the counter, a tall man with a ponytail walked into the store.

'I'm afraid we're closing,' Otto told him firmly.

'I just want to put a notice on the notice board,' the man said. He was a piano teacher, he explained, flexing his remarkably long fingers. He wanted to use the shop's notice board to advertise piano lessons.

Otto's mother had started the shop's notice board about a year earlier because she decided it would be good for business. 'It will attract more people into the shop and more people in the shop means more books sold,' she had assured Otto enthusiastically.

Unfortunately, the last part of her logic was

flawed. More people in the shop did not mean more books sold, since most of the people who used the notice board were as poor as church mice. Sometimes they took a book off the shelves and stood there for ages reading it, but they hardly ever bought anything. Nevertheless, Otto's mother always insisted that the notice board was a great success.

'How much does it cost to advertise?' the piano teacher asked.

Otto hesitated. He had no idea what his mother charged. All he could think about was getting the man out of the shop. Finally he said, 'It's free today.'

The piano teacher looked surprised. He handed over the card on which he had written his advertisement and left the shop. Finally, Otto got a chance to lock the door.

Thank goodness! he thought to himself.

He looked for a place on the notice board to pin up the piano teacher's card. There was just one empty space, in the bottom right-hand corner beside an advertisement for labrador puppies in need of good homes, and one for something called 'The Magical Detective Agency'.

Otto blinked. The Magical Detective Agency? He didn't remember seeing that before. He took the card down and studied it more carefully. At the top was a five-pointed star with the letters *MDA* written in the centre. Below that was written:

The Magical Detective Agency
Magical Crimes Investigated
Supernatural Mysteries Solved.

At the bottom was the name Maximillian Hawksmoor and an address on the other side of town.

Otto unpinned the card and studied it carefully. Was this the solution he was looking for? After all, there was something very strange about his mother's disappearance – the atmosphere in the shop, his mother's face in the mirror.

But what if it was a trick of some kind – a way of conning desperate people out of their money? Or worse still, what if it had something to do with his mother's disappearance?

Well there was only one way to find out.

2

THE TROUBLE WITH CATS

Juliet Pennington was a very down-to-earth girl who generally behaved with a great deal of common sense. So why was she looking for a book about training cats? The explanation was quite simple. Earlier that day, she had come back from a friend's house to find her cat, Corny, in serious trouble.

Corny, or Cornelius to give him his full name, was a big, solid-looking black cat with a tail as thick as your arm. Everything about him suggested an animal in the prime of health. But Cornelius had not always looked like this. He had turned up meowing piteously on the doorstep of Juliet's house on the morning of her seventh birthday, looking half-starved, flea-bitten and uncared for. As soon as she saw him, Juliet had decided to take him under her wing. Her parents had not been terribly keen on the idea but Juliet could be very determined when she needed to be. So, they eventually gave way and Cornelius became the family cat.

Unfortunately, Corny repaid this hospitality by causing as much trouble as possible, sharpening his claws on the sofa, leaving hairs on the beds, and sleeping in the ironing basket. Recently, his trouble-making had reached new heights when he had begun sneaking into Belsham Manor – the nearby stately home where Juliet's father worked as a gardener – and stealing things. In the last fortnight he had turned up at the back door with two odd socks, a fur mitten, and a rather ancient looking black hat with a veil at the front. Juliet was obliged to return all these items to their owner with profuse apologies.

Earlier that morning, Juliet had walked through the front door, hung up her coat and made her way to the kitchen where she had just finished pouring herself a glass of orange juice when her mother came in carrying a load of dirty washing.

'That cat of yours has been causing trouble again,' her mother announced crossly, stuffing the dirty washing into the washing machine so fiercely that Juliet suspected she would have liked to put Corny in there as well.

Juliet sighed. 'What's he done this time?' she asked.

'He pinched a fish that was intended for Miss Honoria's dinner,' her mother replied, standing up and looking sternly at Juliet over an armful of sheets and pillowcases.

'Oh dear!' Miss Honoria was the owner of Belsham Manor. She was also Juliet's father's employer.

'Miss Honoria was very upset about it,' Juliet's mother continued. 'She'd taken the bus into town specially to buy that fish and now she's too exhausted to go in again to get another.'

'I'll get some for her,' Juliet volunteered.

'That's all very well,' her mother continued, 'but it makes things very difficult for your father. Something has got to be done about that cat.'

'Like what?'

'I don't know. But either Cornelius learns to behave himself or he has to go. Do you understand?'

'Yes, Mum.'

And that was why, when Juliet turned up at

Spinoza's second-hand bookshop half-an-hour later she was looking for a book on training cats. As it turned out, there was absolutely nothing in the bookshop about cats. The only book that looked even remotely useful was one called *The Obedient Dog*, because it had a chapter entitled 'Animal Psychology'. Juliet leafed through the pages and shook her head. She couldn't imagine Cornelius behaving like the dog in the photographs, but she decided to give it a try.

Then she looked at the books about Ancient Rome. A few days earlier, her father had found an odd-looking old coin while digging over Miss Honoria's flowerbeds. He had thought it might be Roman and had given it to Juliet.

There was only one book with a chapter devoted to coins. She took it to the counter, along with *The Obedient Dog*.

After visiting the bookshop, she went to the fishmonger and bought the fish. Then she set off home up the hill.

She knocked on the door of Belsham Manor and after a very long time a small white-haired old lady opened the door. This was Miss Honoria.

Juliet handed her the fish. 'I'm terribly sorry about my cat,' she said. 'I'll try to make sure he doesn't do it again.'

Miss Honoria smiled. 'Thank you very much, my dear,' she said. 'I do love a nice piece of fish.'

So does Corny, Juliet thought to herself, but she decided that the less said about that the better. Miss Honoria was a nice old lady, really; other people might have made more of a fuss. So she just smiled and said goodbye. She went back home, took a chair out into the garden and sat down to study *The Obedient Dog*.

'A trained dog is a happy and fulfilled animal,' Juliet read, 'but you should always remember that even the smartest animals cannot really understand human speech. Nevertheless, dogs are certainly more intelligent than cats.'

Juliet looked up from the book. Cornelius was lying on the grass, sunning himself. As she watched, he stretched and yawned. He wouldn't think much of that comment, she decided.

She turned back to the book and read on. The first thing to do when training any animal, she learned, was to make it understand that you are in charge. Animals understand dominance and you must let them know that you are the boss. When training a dog, you begin by teaching it to come to heel.

Juliet closed the book. Why shouldn't it work with a cat? Some cats might not be as clever as dogs but she was convinced that Corny was extremely intelligent. Sometimes when he looked at her, she almost expected him to talk. She stood up, marched over to Cornelius and picked him up.

He looked greatly affronted.

'Now then, Corny, when I say heel, I want you to stand still beside me,' she declared, putting him down on the ground next to her.

The moment she let him go, Cornelius raced off.

'Come back Corny, you bad cat!' Juliet cried, hurrying after him.

But Cornelius had no intention of coming back. He shot through the hedge and into the grounds of Belsham Manor. Juliet opened the garden gate and ran after him. He was a long way ahead of her by now, over by the wall at the far end of the ground. Beside this wall was an immense and very ancient horse chestnut tree. Cornelius shot up the tree and sat on a branch mid-way up, waving his tail back and forth angrily. He gazed down haughtily at Juliet for a moment before leaping off the branch and disappearing over the other side of the wall.

But this wall was not the end of the grounds. Originally, the lawns and terraces of Belsham Manor had been much larger. They had been looked after by a head gardener and three under-gardeners. But over the years, the Belsham fortune had dwindled until there came a point when there was not enough money left to pay four men's wages. So the owners of the house had built a wall about a third of the way along and left the other two thirds of the garden to look after itself. Nobody bothered about the abandoned area any longer and in time it had become a complete wilderness. It was into this forgotten jungle that Cornelius had jumped.

Juliet was not the kind of girl to give up easily. 'If that cat thinks he's got away from me, he's in for a big surprise,' she muttered to herself.

There was a low door in the wall that led into the forgotten section of the garden. Juliet had tried to open it on many occasions in the past but she had never been able to budge it. But there's a first time for everything, she thought to herself. Lifting the latch, she pushed with all her strength.

Nothing happened.

'I'm not going to let it beat me!' she declared. Planting her feet firmly on the ground, she put her shoulder to the door and shoved.

Was she imagining it or had it moved a fraction of an inch?

She tried again, groaning out loud with the effort. Suddenly, the door burst open and Juliet tumbled into the forgotten garden.

3

MAXIMILLIAN HAWKSMOOR

Otto had run all the way to the street where the Magical Detective Agency was located. But now that he was actually standing on the doorstep, he hesitated. Even if it wasn't a trick, whoever ran the agency might decide to go straight to the authorities once they'd heard his story. Police officers and social workers would get involved. They might decide that his mother was not a fit and proper person to look after him. Her greatest fear would turn out to be well-founded.

But on the other hand, he couldn't manage this by himself.

He rang the doorbell. A few moments later it was opened by a tall, thin man. To look at his face, you might think he was no more than thirty-five. But there was something about his manner that made him seem much older, or as if he came from an earlier time.

He was dressed in a tweed jacket, open-necked shirt and flannel trousers. He had the blackest hair that Otto had ever seen, with thick bushy eyebrows like two furry caterpillars crawling across his brow. His nose was prominent and slightly curved, making him look a little like a bird of prey, a resemblance that was increased by the fierce intelligence that burned behind his clear blue eyes.

It was those eyes that made the biggest impression on Otto. Looking into them, he immediately had the feeling that the man who stood before him was someone quite out of the ordinary, someone who could do things that other people had no idea were possible.

'Can I help you?' the owner of that remarkable gaze now asked.

'I'm looking for Maximillian Hawksmoor,' Otto replied.

'Well you've found him. May I ask your business?'

'My mother has disappeared.'

Maximillian Hawksmoor raised one bushy eyebrow. 'You'd better come in then.'

He led Otto into the hall and up a flight of steps to the first floor.

'This is my consulting room,' Maximillian declared, opening the door to a moderate sized room in which a couple of big old leather armchairs were ranged in front of a coal fire. There was a Turkish rug on the floor and the walls were lined with bookshelves from floor to ceiling. The curtains were drawn and, to Otto's surprise, there was no electric light. Instead, four tall candelabras stood in each corner of the room.

'Perhaps you'd care for a cup of tea and a slice of cake?' Maximillian suggested. 'I was just about to have some myself.'

Otto was about to say that he would much rather not waste any time when he suddenly realised that he was extremely hungry. He'd only had a bowl of cornflakes for breakfast and it was well past his lunch time. 'Thank you,' he said.

Maximillian disappeared and Otto took the opportunity to look around the room more carefully. There were almost as many books as in his mother's shop, but the volumes which filled these shelves were very old and bound in leather. The names on some were in languages that Otto did not recognise. Nevertheless, he knew enough to guess that the library was worth a fortune.

In a small glass-fronted cabinet, an odd assortment of objects was displayed, including a human skull with a small hole drilled neatly through the top, a dagger with half the blade broken off, a silver goblet, three porcupine quills, and an old clay pipe.

'Souvenirs from some of my cases,' Maximillian remarked, placing a tray with a teapot, two cups and saucers and two large slices of cake on a small table between the two chairs. 'Please sit down and tell me all about yourself.'

They sat and Maximillian poured out the tea. Above the fireplace, a portrait of a rather severe looking gentleman in a frock coat stared down at them with such a fierce look that Otto had to force himself to look away.

Otto sipped the tea – which was very hot – and took a bite of cake. It tasted remarkably good. When he had finished eating, he began to describe his predicament. He was halfway through describing what had happened when he glanced down. To his surprise, the pattern on the carpet appeared to be moving. He stopped what he was saying and stared. Was it the shadows thrown by the flickering candle flames, or were the plants and animals beneath his feet writhing and wriggling as if they were alive?

'You were saying?' Maximillian's request forced Otto to look up again.

'The carpet…' Otto said. 'It's—'

'Very old,' Maximillian interrupted. 'It comes from a place called Quillipoth. But you were telling me about your mother.'

I must have imagined it, Otto told himself. And with all that he'd been through it was not so surprising that his mind might have begun to play tricks. Pulling himself together, he continued with his account of his mother's disappearance and when hc happened to glance at the floor again the carpet was behaving like any other carpet in any other room.

Nevertheless, Otto still felt confused and uncertain about everything. The room, for example. When he had first walked in it had appeared to be no bigger than the sitting room in the apartment he shared with his mother. So why did he keep getting the sensation that he was actually in a much bigger space, like some

31

vast hall in a palace or a temple from ancient times?

Otto forced himself to concentrate as he described the way the air in the bookshop had seemed to crackle with energy, and the feeling of dizziness he had experienced on crossing the threshold, the glimpse of his mother's face in the bedroom mirror and the words he had found spelled out on the refrigerator door.

When the end of the story was reached Maximillian nodded slowly. 'You know, Otto, I think you may be a sensitive!' he said.

'What's a sensitive?' Otto asked, suspiciously.

'A sensitive is someone who reacts to the presence of magic.'

'So you're saying that magic is real?'

'Of course it's real!' Maximillian assured him. 'Isn't that why you're here – because you suspect that whatever has happened to your mother has some magical origin?'

'I don't know why I'm here,' Otto admitted. 'And I have absolutely no idea what has happened to my mother. But it's not like her to disappear without telling me and I just thought you might be able to help. It's true that the sensation I had when I entered the shop *was* very strange. But I'm not sure I really believe in magic.'

Maximillian nodded. 'That's what most people would say. The fact is that we all have a degree of magical awareness, though most people won't admit it. Magic makes them nervous. So they make themselves feel better by laughing about it and assuring themselves that it couldn't possibly exist. Deep down inside they know there's more to the world than ever gets explained on the television, but they convince themselves that it isn't important. Every now and again, however, someone like you comes along, someone whose magical awareness is too strong for him to ignore it. He fights it and fights it until finally he is forced to accept that the only explanation for what is happening is magic.'

Otto considered this. Could it be the reason he had always felt different from other children?

'Now, why don't you tell me about the rest of your family?' Maximillian continued.

Otto shook his head. 'There isn't anyone else.'

'What about your father?'

'He died when I was very young.' Otto explained about the mysterious tropical illness.

'I see,' Maximillian said. 'And there's no one else at all? No brothers or sisters, aunts, uncles or cousins? Not even any friends of the family?'

Otto shook his head. 'I'm alone in the world,' he said. As he said this, a feeling of desperation threatened to engulf him.

Maximillian looked Otto right in the eye and held his gaze for a moment. Then he smiled. 'Not any longer, Otto,' he said, speaking quietly but distinctly. 'We'll find your mother, don't you worry.'

Otto felt profoundly grateful. He was still not sure that he could trust this man. But at least someone was offering to help. Ever since he'd come back to the bookshop to find his mother missing, he'd been struggling to do the right thing and it was so hard when you had to make all the decisions by yourself.

Then he remembered that they had not yet discussed money. Otto did have some money that his mother had given him for his birthday, but he suspected it would not buy very much of a private investigator's time.

'You haven't told me how much you charge,' he said.

'Well now, that depends on how interested I am,' Maximillian replied, 'I can be very expensive indeed.'

Otto's heart sank.

'As it happens, I am particularly intrigued by your case,' Maximillian continued. 'Consequently, my fee would be one penny per day.'

Otto stared at him in astonishment. 'One penny per day!' he exclaimed. 'But that's ridiculous.'

Maximillian raised one thick black eyebrow. 'Some people would say that the whole idea of a magical detective agency is ridiculous, especially in Bridlington Chawley. But here I am, all the same.' He held out his hand. 'Is it a deal?

Otto was just about to shake hands with the magical detective when he stopped, noticing that the hand Maximillian offered him had six fingers.

Maximillian followed the direction of Otto's gaze and nodded. 'Two middle fingers,' he said. 'My father had the same thing. That's his portrait above the fireplace. And so did his father. Probably *his* father too for all I know. You needn't worry. It's just a genetic peculiarity. I'm not a werewolf or anything.'

He continued to sit there, smiling, with his hand extended. After a moment, Otto put out his own hand and they shook on the deal.

'And now, I think we need to gather some evidence,' Maximillian said. 'The next step, therefore, is for me to take a look around the bookshop. Shall we go? My car is in the garage.'

He put on a long coat that had been hanging on a peg beside the door and picked up a small leather bag, like the kind that doctors sometimes carry. 'Ready?' he asked.

'What about the fire? Is it safe to leave it blazing away like this?' Otto asked. 'And the candles? Shouldn't you put them out?'

Otto's mother had a horror of fires. She would not allow a single candle in the house and she checked the smoke alarm at least once a week. 'A bookshop is a bonfire waiting for a match,' she often told him. The same could clearly be said of Maximillian's consulting room, with its shelves and shelves of leather bound volumes.

'Oh, don't worry about that,' Maximillian replied. 'This room is protected.'

Protected in what way, Otto wondered? A sprinkler system perhaps. He glanced up at the ceiling.

'Enchantments, Otto,' Maximillian told him, 'of the very strongest kind. Now come on, let's not waste another moment.'

The car that waited in the shadows of Maximillian's garage was bright red, with an open top and gleaming chrome work. Even with the engine turned off, it seemed to be straining at the leash, ready to bound up the road like a thoroughbred racehorse.

Maximillian chuckled to himself when they were both strapped into their seats. 'I do so enjoy the beginning of a new case,' he said. Then he turned on the engine and took off the hand brake. As they shot down the road at quite an alarming speed, Otto wondered what on Earth he had got himself into.

4

HUNCHABILITY

Maximillian stood in the middle of the bookshop, sniffing the air like a bloodhound seeking a scent. 'No doubt about it! There's definitely been some sort of magical activity going on here,' he announced. 'The place positively reeks of it.'

He took a magnifying glass out of his pocket, got down on his hands and knees and began examining the floor in great detail.

'What are you looking for?' Otto asked. Despite shaking hands with Maximillian, he was still unsure what he really thought of the man.

'Clues,' Maximillian replied. 'Every contact leaves a trace. It's just a matter of knowing how to recognise it. Aha! What have we here?' He pointed to a greyish-green smudge on the mat just inside the doorway.

'Looks like a bit of dirt, to me,' Otto observed. 'I don't see how that's going to help. It could

38

have come from anybody's shoe, including yours or mine.'

Maximillian shook his head. 'This dirt, as you call it, Otto, is actually sand, but not just any sand. No, as far as I know, sand of this particular greenish colour is only to be found in one location.'

'And where's that?'

'The sand dunes of Quillipoth.'

'Isn't that where you got your carpet?'

'Exactly.' Maximillian reached into his bag and brought out a small glass jar and a tiny brush. He carefully swept a few grains of the green sand into the container, screwed on the lid and put it in his pocket. Then he straightened up. 'I think we need to carry out an etheric fragmentation test,' he said.

'What's that?'

Maximillian frowned. 'Let me see, how shall I put it? I know. Try to imagine that the world, and by the world I mean not just the Earth but the entire universe, is really an egg.'

'Like the ones that come in packets of six in the supermarket?'

'Exactly. Only much, much bigger. Can you do that?'

'I think so.'

'Good. Now imagine that there is not just one of these eggs but a great many of them.'

'So you're saying that there's more than one world?'

'You catch on fast, Otto. Now picture those eggs lying in a bowl on the kitchen table. Some of them are touching other eggs. Some of them are not. Our egg, by which I mean of course our world, is one of those touching another. The two eggs are contingent, to use the technical term. Are you with me so far?'

'I suppose so,' Otto agreed, 'but I don't see how all this is helping us find my mother.'

'Patience,' Maximillian replied. 'Now then, like those eggs, the world that we inhabit is surrounded by a kind of shell, only the world's shell is made of something that magicians call 'ether'. It cannot be seen, it cannot be touched, it cannot even be measured. But it's there, just the same. And all the other worlds have their own shells, too.'

'Most of the time these etheric shells keep the contents of the different worlds separate from each other. That's what they're for, you see. But every now and again something or somebody passes from one world to another. Sometimes by accident, sometimes on purpose. When that happens, the etheric shell is damaged, or fragmented, slightly.'

'I see,' Otto said, though he wasn't sure he did really. 'So how do we test for this etheric fragmentation?'

'We cast a spell.' Maximillian said, as if it was the sort of thing people did all the time. 'Not a very strong one, obviously. We don't want to draw attention to ourselves, in case there are any unsavoury characters hanging about. A simple revealing spell should do the trick.'

'What sort of unsavoury characters might be hanging about?' Otto asked, looking nervously over his shoulder.

'The kind that kidnap bookshop owners,' Maximillian told him. 'Now then, let's get started. He put his hand in his pocket, took out a small paper bag and held it out towards Otto. 'Sherbet lemon?'

'Sorry?'

'Have a sherbet lemon. I find them very helpful when casting magic spells. Stops your mouth from getting too dry.'

'Thanks,' Otto said. He took one of the sweets

and put it in his mouth. Maximillian did the same. Then the magical detective reached into his leather bag and took out a glass salt cellar with a chrome lid, the kind you sometimes see on tables in cafés.

'This is one of the first spells I learned,' he said, pouring salt onto the counter. 'I must have been about your age at the time. You should pay attention. It's very satisfying when it works properly.'

He put the salt cellar back in his bag and spread the grains of salt out. Then he began chanting very quietly. The words, if they were words, were not in English and though Otto tried hard to distinguish them, they all blurred into one. At the same time, Maximillian began passing his left hand, with its six long fingers, backwards and forwards over the salt.

After about a minute of this, the room started to get uncomfortably hot and the back of Otto's neck began itching dreadfully. He was on the point of reaching around to scratch it when there was a smell like gunpowder, and, without anyone touching them, the grains of salt all began to move about, lining up in patterns.

Maximillian clapped his hands together and

beamed delightedly. 'There you are!' he said. 'You must admit that's a very nice result.'

Otto was too surprised to make any kind of response to this, but Maximillian didn't seem to need an answer anyway. 'Look at the fragmentation lines!' he continued enthusiastically. 'There can't be any doubt about it. Someone from a contingent world has been trespassing into ours. And that trespass happened right here in this shop.'

'And you think this has got something to do with my mother's disappearance?'

'No doubt about it. Your mother's been kidnapped by creatures from that other world.'

'What sort of creatures?'

'Elementals, my dear Otto.'

'Elementals?'

'Yes, creatures like us in many ways but uglier, greedier, nastier and with a much more highly developed magical awareness.'

'But why would they want my mother?'

'That's an interesting question,' Maximillian replied. 'And I'm afraid I haven't the slightest idea what the answer might be.'

'But you do know where they came from, right? So we can go after them?'

'Unfortunately, it's not quite that easy. First we have to get into their world, and that means casting a spell.'

'Like with the salt.'

'That was no more than a simple incantation with a few hand gestures,' Maximillian replied. 'A spell to enter another world will need to be much more elaborate. And we certainly can't do it here.'

'Why not?'

'Atmosphere, Otto. Atmosphere! Magic depends on it. Without the right atmosphere you're wasting your time. For example, you can't cast a spell if there's a television on in the room. Did you know that?'

Otto shook his head.

'The television totally ruins the atmosphere. In fact, anything electrical tends to interfere with the magical process. Even those.' He pointed to the fluorescent lights above their heads. 'It's one thing performing a simple incantation but it's quite another trying to magic yourself right out of this world and into another. You need somewhere wild and primitive for that. Like Stonehenge, although that gets awfully crowded these days.'

'But I thought you said the elementals came through here, in this shop. Wasn't that what the fragmentation test proved?'

'That's perfectly true but that sort of thing is a great deal easier for elementals. They are magical by nature. Even the least powerful of them can perform quite advanced magic simply by thinking about it. Whereas we humans have to use spells, rituals, incantations and all sorts of mumbo jumbo.'

'So what do we do next?' Otto asked.

'I need more information before I can answer that with certainty,' Maximillian told him. 'It would help if I could understand how your mother got mixed up in all this in the first place. I don't suppose she kept a diary by any chance?'

Otto nodded. 'She did as a matter of fact, but I've already looked in it. There aren't any clues.'

'Looking and observing are not always the same thing. If you don't mind, therefore, I'd like to glance at it myself,' Maximillian replied.

Otto shrugged. 'If you like.' He went off to fetch the diary. When he came back he found Maximillian examining the counter with his magnifying glass.

'Looking for fingerprints?' Otto asked.

Maximillian shook his head. 'Elementals don't have fingerprints,' he said. 'But they do sometimes leave traces of slime.'

'Slime? Ugh! I thought you said they were like us, except uglier.'

'They are like us, except uglier and a little bit slimy. Yes, see here.' Maximillian pointed to a small stain on the counter.

'Looks more like chocolate to me,' Otto said. 'My mother's got a bit of an obsession with chocolate biscuits, I'm afraid.'

Maximillian put his nose to the counter and sniffed. 'Perhaps you're right,' he said. 'Now let's have a look at what she's been writing.'

Otto handed over the diary and Maximillian leafed through the pages, reading with remarkable speed. Suddenly he came to a halt. 'Well, well, well!' he exclaimed. 'This is very interesting indeed.'

'I didn't see anything interesting,' Otto replied. 'Just a lot of stuff about birds.'

'Exactly!' Maximillian agreed. 'A lot of stuff about birds. Listen to this, for example. It's from the day before yesterday. *There was a black faced spoonbill in the sycamore tree today*. What do you make of that?'

'I don't make anything of it, except that my mother must have been a lot more interested in birds than I realised.'

'What if I told you that the black faced spoonbill was one of the rarest birds on the planet?' Maximillian went on. He looked as if he were enjoying himself enormously.

'Then I'd say she was very lucky to spot one.'

Maximillian shook his head. 'She couldn't have been that lucky,' he said. 'The black faced spoonbill is only found on a few rocky islands off the coast of North Korea and in the Mai Po Marshes of Hong Kong.'

'Then she must have made a mistake.'

'Perhaps.'

'You obviously don't think so.'

'No, I don't.'

An unpleasant thought occurred to Otto. 'You don't think my mother was going crazy, do you?' he asked.

'Did she seem crazy to you?'

'No!'

'Then I very much doubt that she was. No, Otto, it's my belief that your mother had a feeling she was in danger, a presentiment perhaps, and so she left a message in case something happened to her.'

'Well why didn't she leave one that was a bit easier to find?' Otto demanded, 'and one that made sense?'

'Because if she'd done that, the individuals who kidnapped her would have found it and removed it. Tell me, Otto, have you ever heard of hunchability?'

'No. What is it?'

'Hunchability is the magical detective's best friend. It's what you use when you need to solve a case but you haven't any facts, or any decent leads. It means using your imagination and following wherever it leads.'

'OK,' Otto replied. 'So where exactly does your imagination lead you right now?'

'It leads me to birds,' Maximillian said. 'Where are the books on ornithology?'

'On what?'

'Bird-watching.'

'Oh, right. Over in the far right-hand corner.'

'Come on then,' Maximillian said. 'Let's start looking.'

Otto followed him over to the section on birds. It wasn't very large. Just two and a half shelves in all. Maximillian selected the *Bumper*

Book Of British Birds and began systematically leafing through its pages. Otto took down a book entitled *Attracting Wild Birds To Your Garden* and glanced at the contents page. 'What exactly are we supposed to be looking for?' he asked.

'No idea,' Maximillian replied. 'That's the thing about hunchability. You're always working in the dark.' He put the *Bumper Book Of British Birds* back on the shelf and took down *A Guide To The World's Rarest Birds*.

Rather aimlessly, Otto leafed through the pages of *Attracting Wild Birds To Your Garden*. He had just learned that whereas some birds prefer to feed on the ground, others will only feel safe if they are out of reach of predators when Maximillian cried out, 'Bull's-eye!' and held up a sheet of notepaper with a pencil drawing on one side. 'This was tucked away in the chapter on spoonbills,' he explained. 'Unless I'm very much mistaken, it's a map of the grounds of Belsham Manor. And look, there's a cross just here, where it says *fountain*.'

Otto examined the map. 'This wasn't drawn by my mother,' he said. 'That's not her handwriting.'

'Nevertheless, it was in her possession and she obviously thought it important enough to hide it away. Did she ever mention Belsham Manor to you?'

'Not that I can remember.'

'What do you know about the place?'

'Only what everybody knows – that it was built by Sir Henry Belsham, that he and his family were killed in a fire. I think there's just some elderly relative living there now.'

Maximillian nodded. 'Yes, Miss Honoria Belsham, Sir Henry's great great niece.'

'You don't think *she* might be behind my mother's kidnapping, do you?'

'I doubt it,' Maximillian said. 'I've only met her once or twice but she doesn't strike me as a criminal mastermind. Still, you can't be too careful.' He paused for a moment and seemed deep in thought. Finally, he said, 'Just to be on the safe side, we'd better approach the grounds from the rear. In which case, I need to pay a visit to the butcher's shop.'

'The butcher's shop?'

'Yes.' Maximillian gave Otto a wry smile. 'I have a feeling we're going to need rather a lot of meat.'

5

THE ABANDONED GARDEN

When Maximillian came back from the butcher's shop a few minutes later, he was clutching a plastic bag containing a rather bloody looking package wrapped in paper. He said nothing about what he intended to do with it and Otto could not quite pluck up the courage to ask; but he was worried that the meat was intended for some bloodthirsty magical ritual.

'The garden of Belsham Manor backs onto an old timber yard,' Maximillian said, as they clambered into the car. 'The owners have gone bankrupt so it's all locked up, but if we can get into the yard, we should be able to climb over the back fence and enter the garden that way.'

They set off at breakneck speed and were soon out of the town and driving along a narrow, twisting road that wound steadily uphill. On the way Maximillian talked about the stately home's original owner.

'Sir Henry Belsham was known as Lucky Henry because he never put a foot wrong in business and made a fortune in next to no time. Some people suggested there was more than luck involved. There were even rumours that he'd sold his soul to the devil. Then one day, when he was still a young man, he decided to retire and build a house in Bridlington Chawley. That was when his luck ran out. He'd only lived in the new house for three months when a fire broke out in the East Wing. Sir Henry, his wife and their newly born son were all killed.'

'Do you think it's true?' Otto asked. 'About him selling his soul to the devil, I mean?'

'I wouldn't like to say,' Maximillian replied.

They reached the abandoned timber yard. Behind a high chain-link fence, piles of wood lay scattered about. There was a single-storey building that must have once served as an office, but was now boarded up. Other than that, there was no sign of any activity. At the back of the yard was a high brick wall, behind which Otto glimpsed a line of trees.

Maximillian parked the car in a lay-by where it was screened by some bushes. They both got out.

'The first thing we have to do is get through the fence,' Maximillian said. Clutching the carrier bag full of meat in one hand and his little black bag in the other, he led the way to a corner of the fence. He looked up and down the road and when he was sure no one was in sight, he opened his black bag. 'A good detective never goes anywhere without a few basic tools,' he said. He took a powerful pair of wire cutters out of his bag and began to cut a hole in the fence.

He had not got very far, however, before there was a ferocious barking and the most enormous dog came racing across the yard towards them. Otto was horrified. He had been scared of dogs ever since he was seven years old, when a neighbour's dog bit him after he tried to stroke it. But Maximillian remained perfectly calm. He took the meat out of the carrier bag and reaching into the hole he had just cut, threw the parcel, paper and all, as far as he could.

The dog came to a halt and stood looking suspiciously from Maximillian to the meat. There was obviously a considerable battle going on between its stomach and its brain. Fortunately, the stomach triumphed and the dog ran over to the parcel. But Otto suspected that it would not take very long for the dog to devour the whole lot and he watched anxiously as Maximillian steadily widened the hole.

'Couldn't you just put a spell on the dog?' he suggested.

Maximillian shook his head. 'I'm afraid not. Dogs are completely immune to magic. No one knows why for certain but it's generally thought they simply refuse to believe in it. They're very practical animals, you know. Give them a stick to chase and they're happy, but try to levitate them or change their appearance and they kick up an awful fuss. Now cats are a different matter. Of course they're quite magical animals themselves. In fact, there's a theory that cats are not really from this world at all, that the first cat came here by accident from a contingent world and liked it so much she stayed.'

He stopped cutting the fence and considered the hole he had made. 'Right, that looks big enough now,' he said, putting the wire cutters back in the bag. 'I'll go first. You follow. Once you're through, make for that pile of timber stacked up against the wall at the far end.' With that, he squeezed through the hole and began running across the yard with remarkable speed.

The dog looked up and regarded him with a look of surprised indignation, but luckily for Maximillian the demands of its appetite were too great and it turned its attention back to the meat.

Otto hesitated. He knew that the longer he delayed, the less time he had to get across the yard before the dog finished its meal, but fear held him prisoner.

'Come on, Otto!' Maximillian yelled. He had reached the stack of timber at the far side of the yard and was already beginning to climb it.

Swallowing his terror, Otto pushed through the hole in the fence and set off across the yard. This time the dog did not even raise its head.

There was no great distance for him to cover, yet it seemed to Otto that he would never get there. He could feel his heart thumping in his chest as he ran and every breath seemed to be drawn in over red-hot coals. But at last he reached the stack of timber, on top of which sat Maximillian, urging him on. He looked around for a route upwards and saw that he could use the uneven way the wood had been stacked almost like a ladder. He had only just begun to climb, however, when he heard a ferocious barking coming from behind him. He turned and, to his dismay, saw that the dog was hurtling towards him. His legs turned to jelly.

'Keep climbing!' Maximillian shouted.

But it was too late! Snarling furiously, the dog leapt through the air and closed its jaws around Otto's trouser leg. Otto fought back, kicking with all his might, but the dog held on, dragging him downwards. For a horrible moment, Otto saw himself ending up like the bloody package of meat that Maximillian had brought from the butcher.

Then, suddenly, a bird came swooping out of the sky and plunged straight at the dog. Startled, it released its grip on Otto's trousers and backed away. A moment later another bird plummeted downwards, aiming directly for the dog's face, only swerving away at the very last moment. The dog looked astonished, and began barking furiously, snapping at the empty air. But a moment later the first bird returned, like a bullet. Otto didn't wait to watch any more. He scrambled up the timber stack out of the dog's reach as the two birds repeatedly dive-bombed his canine attacker.

Maximillian was sitting on the top of the woodpile grinning happily.

'What did you do?' Otto asked him, still shaking from his close call.

'I couldn't do anything about the dog so I cast a spell on the birds,' he replied. 'They thought you were a young chick under attack. Plucky little things, aren't they? Come on, let's not waste any more time. We have to get over the wall.'

Otto turned and gazed across at the dense woodland on the other side. 'How are we supposed to do that?' he asked.

'We climb,' Maximillian said. He pointed to where the branches of a horse chestnut tree overhung the wall on their side.

'You can't be serious!' Otto said.

'It's easy,' Maximillian told him. 'Just watch me and do the same,' With that, he threw his bag over the wall, leaned forwards, took hold of one branch and stepped gingerly onto another. Then he edged his way carefully along until, within a few minutes, he was perched in the tree on the other side, leaning against the trunk and looking encouragingly in Otto's direction. 'Your turn,' he called.

Apart from dogs, the only other thing that really scared Otto was heights. But he reminded himself that he was doing this for his mother. So he counted to three, took a deep breath and grabbed hold of the overhanging branch.

It only took a few moments at the most to reach the relative safety of the tree trunk, but they were some of the longest moments of Otto's life. By the time he was clinging onto the trunk beside Maximillian, his whole body was trembling. Now he just had to get down to the ground.

Descending from the tree was by no means straightforward, but compared to what Otto had just been through, it was a piece of cake. Nevertheless, when he finally reached the ground, he was forced to sit with his back to the tree for a few moments until he felt strong enough to stand. In the meantime, Maximillian retrieved his bag, took out the map and studied it carefully.

'This place is like a jungle,' Otto said, looking around in disbelief.

'It's been abandoned for a very long time,' Maximillian told him, 'but according to this map there was a paved courtyard with a fountain at its heart somewhere between here and the house. Of course, trees and bushes will have grown up through the paving stones by now, so it won't be easy to find.' He produced a pocket compass and studied it. 'That way,' he said, pointing straight ahead.

They began to force their way through the undergrowth. Thorns and brambles tore their hands, branches whipped them in the face, tendrils wrapped themselves around their ankles. But at last they emerged into a space that was relatively free of vegetation. Covered in moss and hidden by grass, the shapes of paving stones could still be discerned beneath their feet. In the centre was a great stone basin into which a fountain must once have tumbled.

'This looks like it!' Maximillian said. 'Now all we have to do is find out why your mother thought this place was so important that she hid a map of it in that book.'

'Perhaps you should start with another etheric fragmentation test,' Otto suggested.

'Good idea.' Maximillian cleared away the grass and fallen leaves from one of the flagstones, poured out some salt and began the ritual. Once again, Otto found himself becoming uncomfortably hot. Then there was the same smell, like spent fireworks, and the grains of salt began to move. This time, however, instead of arranging themselves into jagged lines, they moved outwards from the centre to form a perfect circle.

Maximillian gave a low whistle.

'What does that mean?' Otto asked.

'It means that we are standing right in the middle of a Janusian Portal!' Maximillian told him. 'In fact I'd say this fountain was the exact epicentre.'

'That's not really tremendously helpful,' Otto pointed out, 'since I've no idea what a Janusian Portal is.'

'Sorry. I was so excited I forgot,' Maximillian admitted. 'A Janusian Portal is nothing more than a gateway between two worlds. Named after Janus, the Roman god of doorways, who faced both ways at the same time. That's the difficult bit, you see. Anyone can cast a spell and make themselves disappear out of this world. Well, almost anyone. But casting a spell that makes it possible to get out of this world and then back *into* it again in the same place, at the exact same time that you left is a different matter altogether. That's a Janusian portal.'

'So we can use it to find my mother?' Otto said, eagerly.

'Yes. But it's not just a matter of snapping your fingers. A Janusian Portal is basically a subliminal magical field that has been rendered effectively dormant.'

'You're doing it again,' Otto objected.

'Doing what?'

'Talking in words I don't understand.'

'Sorry, but it isn't easy to explain these things without using a few technical terms every now and then. What I'm trying to tell you is that the magic is here, but it's asleep. If we want to use it, first we have to wake it up. Now, let me think. How is this done? Oh yes, I remember. We need to give the magic something to shape itself around so we set up boundary markers at the four points of the compass. They don't need to be elaborate but they do need to be personal.' He reached into his bag, brought out a pair of scissors and held them out to Otto. 'Cut off some of your hair!' he ordered.

'Cut off some of my hair?'

'It doesn't need to be very much. A handful will do.'

Reluctantly, Otto took the scissors and snipped off a part of his fringe.

Maximillian divided the lock of hair into four smaller ones, took a ball of string out of his pocket and, cutting off four short lengths, tied a knot around each of the locks. 'Now then, I'm going to set up the boundary markers,' he said, taking out his compass and consulting it again. He walked twenty paces north from the fountain, placed one of the locks of hair on the ground and weighed it down with a stone. Then he repeated the process at the other three points of the compass.

'Right now, starting at north, I want you to walk anti-clockwise in a circle round all four of the boundary markers three times, singing a song,' he said.

'What song?' Otto asked.

'It doesn't matter. Any song will do. You're just creating an auditory trace that personalises the magic so that it recognises you and acts in response to your wish to find your mother, instantaneously transporting you to her location. Otherwise, it might decide not to work. Magic can be a bit moody sometimes.'

'But I can't think of any songs,' Otto objected.

'All right then, chant a nursery rhyme.'

'A nursery rhyme! How old do you think I am?' Otto said indignantly.

'I didn't know there was an age limit on nursery rhymes,' Maximillian said. 'Look, you must know something you can chant? Poetry. How about that?'

'I know the witches' speech from *Macbeth*,' Otto said. 'We did it at school.'

'Perfect! Just keep chanting it and don't stop until you've gone round three times. At the same time I will cast the opening spell. Are you ready?'

'I think so.'

'Good. Off you go. Remember anti-clockwise.'

'What would happen if I went clockwise?'

'It would probably kill us both.'

Otto made his way over to the north boundary marker and began to walk in an anti-clockwise circle, chanting, 'Hubble, bubble, toil and trouble, fire burn and cauldron bubble.'

As he did this, he watched Maximillian who was standing beside the fountain with his eyes closed, muttering to himself in that same language he had used when passing his hands over the salt. At first nothing much seemed to happen and Otto began to feel extremely silly. But then the basin of the fountain seemed to fill with liquid light – until it was brimming over. And now the light began to flow outwards from the fountain like a luminous mist, bathing the magical detective in unearthly brilliance, reaching out in a great wave towards Otto who found that he was hypnotized by the light and could not take his eyes off it.

And that was why neither Otto nor Maximillian noticed when a rather well-fed black cat with a particularly fine tail came rushing out of the bushes, closely followed by a girl who was calling out, 'Corny, come back here this minute!'

A moment later all four of them vanished right out of the garden.

6

THROUGH THE PORTAL

There was a noise like a giant zip being unfastened and Otto felt as if his stomach had been turned inside out. Fortunately, this sensation did not last very long and when it was over he found himself standing on a stretch of greenish sand, beside a slate-blue ocean. Where the fountain had been, there was a lump of smooth black rock sticking out of the sand. Above him, the sun blazed down from a deep blue sky, with just a few small wispy clouds dotted here and there. Behind him was an expanse of sand dunes in which a few tired looking clumps of grass had attempted to establish a foothold. It was very hot. Wherever he was, it certainly wasn't Bridlington Chawley.

The beach stretched as far as the eye could see and was entirely empty, except for three other figures. Standing opposite him was Maximillian with his eyes closed, his arms still raised in the air and his black bag by his side. Not far away, with one foot off the ground and one arm outstretched as if she had been frozen in the act of running was…Juliet Pennington! What on earth was she doing here? And not far from Juliet crouched a large black cat, its fur standing on end as if it had just had a rather nasty electric shock.

Otto was still trying to come to terms with all this when Juliet staggered forwards slightly, as if she had just stepped off an escalator and missed her footing. She righted herself and looked around rather crossly. 'What's going on?' she demanded.

Maximillian opened his eyes, saw Juliet and the cat, and made a rather cross face. 'You've just gate-crashed our Janusian Portal,' he told her. 'That's what's going on.'

'Gate-crashed your what?'

'What the magician is trying to say,' the cat declared in a rich, dark chocolatey sort of voice, 'is that he has transported us all out of our world and into this world.'

Both Otto and Juliet stared at the cat in astonishment. It was Juliet who spoke first. 'You can talk!' she declared.

'Well, of course I can talk,' the cat replied.

'But you've never spoken before.'

'You mean you've never understood me before. It's not the same thing at all.' With that, the cat lifted one leg in the air and began washing itself.

'This is a dream,' Juliet told herself. 'I'm going to wake up in a minute.'

'I'm afraid it isn't a dream,' Maximillian assured her. 'It's all perfectly real.'

'It can't be,' Juliet insisted. 'For one thing, cats can't talk. That's just ridiculous.'

The cat paused in its washing and regarded her with unblinking eyes. 'I'll tell you what's ridiculous,' it said after a moment or two. 'Expecting me to come to heel like a canine is ridiculous.' It shuddered. 'The very idea!'

'Look, I'm terribly sorry about this,' Maximillian said. 'I'll send you both back right away.'

'Nobody's sending me anywhere,' the cat replied. 'I didn't ask to be brought here but now that I *am* here, I'm going to explore, just as soon as I've finished washing. That's what cats do, after all. We are independent creatures. We don't chase sticks, we don't come to heel, but we *do* explore. And this is a much more interesting place to explore than the garden of Belsham Manor.'

'But it might not be a very safe place,' Maximillian pointed out. 'Curiosity killed the cat, remember?'

The cat tutted loudly. 'That's such an unoriginal thing to say,' he pointed out.

'What do you mean, this isn't a very safe place?' Juliet demanded.

'Yes, what *do* you mean?' Otto added, looking around anxiously.

'I'd rather not stand around discussing it on this beach where anyone can see us,' Maximillian said. 'I really think it would be best if I sent this young lady and her cat back home right away. Then Otto and I can go about our business.'

'Firstly, I am not her cat,' the cat replied, 'any more than she is my human. Secondly, as I've already made plain, I shall leave this place when I choose and not before.'

'And I'm not going anywhere without him,' Juliet added, stubbornly.

'Oh, very well. On your heads be it,' Maximillian said with a sigh, 'but at least let's go somewhere a little less conspicuous.'

'Such as where?' Otto asked.

'We should be reasonably safe amid the sand dunes,' Maximillian said.

There was general agreement to this suggestion. Or, at least, Otto and Juliet agreed and the cat did not disagree. So, with Maximillian in the lead, the company set off across the sand.

Amid the sand dunes, bright blue dragonflies as big as birds darted back and forth with an angry buzzing noise like a super-charged wasp. 'It's all right,' Maximillian said, 'They won't harm you as long as you leave them alone.'

Cornelius eyed them with interest. 'I wonder what they would be like to eat,' he said.

'Very nasty, I should think,' Maximillian told him. 'Elementals use them to make a kind of deadly poison.'

'Haven't we gone far enough from the beach yet?' Juliet said. 'It's so hot!'

'Oh, very well. I suppose this is as good as anywhere,' Maximillian conceded as they all flopped down in a dip between the dunes.

'Now perhaps you'll tell me exactly what's going on,' Juliet said, 'starting with where on earth we are and why my cat...'

The cat cleared its throat noisily.

'And why Cornelius can now talk, or at least why we can all understand him.'

'Well, I'll try,' Maximillian agreed. 'But you may find it a bit confusing at first. Let me begin by introducing myself. My name is Maximillian Hawksmoor and I am a magical detective, which means that I investigate crimes that have a magical element to them. This place to which you have been transported is nowhere on Earth, I'm afraid. It's another world, and I don't mean another country, or another continent, or even another planet. I'm talking about an entirely different world, one which can only be reached by magic.

'The name of this world is Quillipoth and the creatures who live here are known as elementals. Not all of them are very nice. In fact many of them are thoroughly nasty, which was why I was so anxious to get off the beach where anybody might see us.

'As for why we can now understand Cornelius, I suspect it's a side effect of the magic which allowed us to enter this world. You see, a Janusian Portal is really a very large spell made up of a number of smaller spells, one of which provides the travellers with instantaneous comprehension of whatever language is spoken in the world they are entering. In this case, the effect seems to have included Cornelius as well.'

'All right,' Juliet said. 'I'm not saying I believe you but it sort of makes sense, I suppose. But what are *you* doing here, Otto?'

Otto described how his mother had gone missing and how he had contacted the magical detective agency. 'Maximillian found some clues, which made him think my mother had been kidnapped and brought here. Then he discovered a map of the grounds of Belsham Manor, which my mother had hidden in a book, and that led us to the fountain where we discovered the Janusian Portal, which is what transported us all here.'

'Now I think it's time you told us about yourself,' Maximillian said. 'You seem to know Otto already, for example. I hope this isn't some sort of conspiracy.'

'Of course it's not a conspiracy,' Juliet said. 'My name is Juliet Pennington and I know Otto because I'm in his class at school. I live in a house inside the grounds of Belsham Manor and I was in the garden, where I had every right to be, looking for my cat, Cornelius, when all of a sudden there was a flash of light and I found myself here.'

'I do wish you'd stop referring to me as *your* cat,' said Cornelius. 'It's so vulgar.' He stretched each of his legs, then turned to Maximillian and said, 'Look, this has obviously happened for a reason. When it comes to magic, there's no such thing as coincidence. Even a human like you must realise that.' Maximillian opened his mouth to protest but Cornelius didn't give him a chance to speak. 'We're obviously meant to be part of this adventure,' he continued. 'So I suggest you tell us how exactly you plan to find Otto's mother?'

Maximillian looked from Cornelius to Juliet. 'Does that go for you, too?' he asked.

Juliet frowned. 'I'm not sure. I want to know how long it's likely to take, first. If I'm not home in time for tea my mum and dad are going to be very cross indeed.'

'You needn't worry about that,' Maximillian assured her. 'However much time we spend here, when we return to our own world it will be exactly the same moment that we left. That's the beauty of a Janusian Portal.'

'Oh good! Then, I agree with Corny,' Juliet said. 'You can count me in.'

'You still haven't told us how you plan to find my mother,' Otto pointed out.

'Well,' Maximillian began, 'to be perfectly honest, I don't really know. The thing is, she could be anywhere in this world and we can't just start looking for her at random. It would be like searching for a needle in a haystack. Only in this case the haystack would be the size of a universe. No, what we need is information, and that means contacts.'

'You must have some contacts here,' Otto pointed out. 'You said you got the carpet in your consulting room from here.'

Maximillian nodded. 'Quite true,' he agreed. 'It was sold to me by an individual named Urt. He's ugly, dirty, smelly, untrustworthy, unreliable, corrupt, treacherous and devious, but if there's any kind of plot going on involving our world and this one, he's more than likely to know about it.'

'How can you be so sure?' Juliet asked.

'Because he's a Gallivant. That is what the creatures who live in this world call one of their number who spends his time moving between worlds and generally causing trouble of one kind or another. That's how I met him, actually. He was wandering around a railway station in London pretending to be human.'

'How did you know he wasn't human?' Cornelius demanded.

'Elementals don't have shadows,' Maximillian said, 'and they also have a tendency to leave slime behind when they touch things. It oozes out of their pores.'

'How disgusting!' Juliet said.

'They sound worse than dogs!' Cornelius observed.

'Oh, they are,' Maximillian replied. 'Dogs can be loyal, friendly and willing to please. Elementals are mostly cruel, envious, and resentful. They are quite incapable of feelings like sympathy or friendship. Some of them understand that these things exist and are rather curious about them. Indeed, I believe that was what Urt was doing in the railway station when I came upon him, looking for people being nice to each other.'

'Why would he want to do that if he wasn't capable of such feelings himself?' Otto asked.

'I got the impression that he drew some sort of satisfaction from it.'

'He can't be all bad then,' Juliet observed.

'No one is all bad, even an elemental,' Maximillian replied. 'But don't get the wrong idea, Juliet. The reason Urt liked to watch people being pleasant to each other was that he seemed to have found a way of siphoning off a little of that energy for himself.'

'Like an emotional parasite?' Otto suggested.

'Precisely.'

'I'd rather we didn't talk about parasites if you don't mind,' Cornelius said. 'We cats have to put up with them all the time – fleas, worms and goodness knows what else. You've no idea how tedious it gets.'

'You know, I think it might be a good idea when we're among the elementals if you were to behave more like a traditional cat,' Maximillian suggested, gently.

'A traditional cat!' Cornelius repeated indignantly. 'And just what is that supposed to mean?'

'It means that you restrict yourself to miaowing and purring,' Maximillian went on. 'And before you object, just listen for a minute.

If they know you can talk, they'll be careful what they say in front of you. But if they don't, they might let anything slip. You could be our secret weapon.'

'I think it sounds like a good idea, Corny,' Juliet observed.

'Please, Cornelius,' Otto said, 'you'd be ever so useful.'

'I'll think about it,' Cornelius said, 'but I'm not promising anything.'

'Anyway,' Maximillian went on, 'I do know this much: Urt lives in the city of Abirkadash, which lies on the other side of these sand dunes, and although he didn't give me his precise address, I expect we could track him down if we were to look in the seediest, most squalid part of the city.'

'Well, I must say, it's not much of a plan,' Cornelius remarked. 'He might not know anything at all.'

'Do you have a better idea?

Cornelius was silent.

'Right then,' Maximillian continued. 'Before we go any further, I want Juliet and Cornelius to think very hard about what they're getting themselves into. Otto is here to rescue his mother. I'm here because it's my job to help him. But there's no need for anyone else to go risking their lives, whatever Cornelius says about coincidence. Abirkadash is an extremely dangerous place and it's quite possible that we may not all get out of there alive. So this is your last chance to back out. Just say the word and I'll send you back to our world.' He looked at them each in turn.

Neither of them said anything.

'Very well then. It's Abirkadash next stop. But don't say I didn't warn you!'

7

CHRISTMAS CAROLS

'The people of Quillipoth are much more varied in appearance than humans,' Maximillian said as they made their way through the dunes. 'Some of them, like Urt for example, would pass unnoticed in the average shopping mall back home. But there are others who look quite unlike us. So when you encounter them, I strongly advise you not to stare.'

'Do they know about us?' Otto asked, 'apart from Gallivants, like Urt, I mean.'

'Oh yes,' Maximillian replied. 'But on the whole they think of us rather as we think of characters in fairy tales. In other words, most of them don't believe we exist at all.'

They were coming to the end of the dunes so they paused for a rest. The sand beneath their feet had given way to a reddish-brown earth and before them stretched a wide, empty plain dotted here and there with spindly trees. In the distance they could see a walled city shimmering in a heat haze. Within the perimeter of the wall, domes, towers, and monuments of every kind jostled for space. To their left the land rose in a series of wooded hills and from this direction an endless line of carts, pulled by horses and oxen, were making their way along a winding road towards the city.

'They don't look very technologically advanced,' Otto remarked.

Maximillian shook his head. 'They're not very good at technology,' he agreed. 'Mostly they rely on magic. But you'd be surprised what they can do, so don't get too cocky.'

They had to walk for another hour before they joined the road that led to the city gates, and when they did, they found themselves part of a very odd procession indeed. They saw elementals with faces that were part human, part dog, others with enormous ears or long thin noses like elephants' trunks, and other still with scaly skin like reptiles, or feathers on their heads instead of hair. Some were much taller than a man, some were as small as children, yet still clearly adults.

Directly in front of them was a group of elementals with hairy faces. One of them had a long tail decorated with ribbons. Cornelius seemed fascinated by this, following every wave or twitch it made. Otto worried that he might make some remark that would cause an incident but, thankfully, he remained silent.

The clothes the elementals wore were as unpredictable as their appearance. Some sported colourful robes embroidered with gold and silver or studded with precious stones; others were dressed very plainly in hooded tunics. There seemed to be no general rule about what was or was not fashionable.

As they drew closer to the gates, the smell of the city grew stronger. On the surface it seemed to be a mixture of cow dung, fried onions and old socks, but underneath there was a hint of something sweeter, more exotic but also slightly sickening. None of the elementals seemed bothered by it. Indeed, Otto saw the elemental with the tail breathing in deeply and smiling.

'Don't you just love the smell of the city?' he asked his companions.

They nodded eagerly.

Although they were no great distance from

the city walls by now, the line of traffic was moving unbearably slowly.

'What's holding everybody up?' Juliet demanded.

The elemental with the tail turned round and looked at her. 'It's the toll,' he said in a hissing voice that set Juliet's teeth on edge.

Maximillian frowned. 'What toll?' he asked.

The elemental shook his head. 'Where have you been?' he said. 'Don't you hear the news? They've started charging thirty kobols per head to enter the city, animals included. Daylight robbery, that's what it is.'

'I see,' Maximillian said. He looked worried.

'Have you got any money?' Otto asked when the elemental had turned back to his companions.

Maximillian shook his head. 'Not a solitary kobol,' he said.

'How did you manage in the past?' Otto asked. 'I thought you visited this world regularly.'

'I never said that,' Maximillian told him.

'So how many times *have* you been here?'

'Well, once actually.'

'Oh great! What are we going to do now?'

'I don't know. I need to think.'

'When I visited London last summer with my mother, we went on the London Eye,' Juliet said. 'You must have seen it. It's a great big thing like an enormous bicycle wheel with glass capsules.'

'Yes, that's very interesting,' Maximillian said, somewhat tartly, 'but if I could just...'

'The thing is,' Juliet continued, taking no notice of the interruption, 'the queue was enormous and people were ever so cross. Then these buskers came along and started singing and that cheered everyone up enormously. I think they made quite a lot of money.'

'Wait a minute!' Otto said. 'You're not suggesting that we sing to the crowd?'

'Why not?' Juliet said.

'Well for one thing, I don't know any songs,' he told her.

'Yes you do. What about Christmas carols?'

'You can't sing Christmas carols!' Otto said. 'It's only July.'

'So what? We're not in Bridlington Chawley now. I don't suppose they've even heard of Christmas here, have they?'

She looked at Maximillian and he shook his head.

'There you are then. Come on, Otto, don't be so feeble. We'll start with "We Three Kings". I'll do the verses and you can join in with the chorus. All we need is a hat.'

Maximillian opened his bag and brought out a rather battered looking cloth cap. 'Will this do?' he asked.

'Perfect,' Juliet replied. She stepped away from the queue, put back her head and began to sing. 'We three kings of Orient are...'

The reaction was remarkable. Every elemental in the queue turned round and stared, but it was impossible to tell from the expressions on their faces whether they liked what they were hearing or not.

What if singing in public is banned? Otto thought to himself. *What if this is some sort of terrible insult?*

His anxious thoughts were interrupted by a dig in the ribs from Juliet and he realised she had come to the end of the verse. 'Ooh-oh star of wonder, star of night,' he chanted, 'Star with royal beauty bright...'

When they reached the end of the song the elementals stared fixedly at them in complete silence.

'I think they liked us,' Juliet whispered. 'Don't you?'

'I think they might be about to kill us,' Otto replied.

'Let's give them another,' Juliet suggested.

'Do you really think that's wise?'

By way of answer, Juliet threw back her head and began to sing "Rudolf the Red Nosed Reindeer". Otto did his best to join in, even though he knew hardly any of the verses.

The elementals continued to gaze at them without the faintest hint of emotion. It was unnerving. *If they don't react in some way at the end of this one, we may have to run away and hide,* Otto thought to himself.

Suddenly their voices were joined by a third – if it could truly be called a voice. Cornelius had begun to produce a dreadful wailing, not unlike the sort of noise you hear when two cats stand facing each other on a garden wall, fur bristling and tails on end. Yet this was clearly not an expression of anger or a declaration of territorial rights. No, in his own shockingly unmusical fashion, Cornelius was joining in with the singing. And the effect on the elementals was electric. Every face in the crowd seemed to light up with pleasure. At the end of the song there was tumultuous applause.

Juliet launched straight into "We Wish You A Merry Christmas" and Cornelius, emboldened by his success, almost drowned her out, keening and caterwauling like a demented banshee.

Juliet went through every carol she could remember, throwing in for good measure a couple of Beatles songs which her mother was accustomed to sing. The elementals were delighted.

When they could think of nothing more to sing, Otto picked up the hat and walked up and down the line holding it out. Coins were dropped in enthusiastically.

'That's a very talented animal you've got there,' an elemental with two small horns and a goatee beard remarked. 'You wouldn't care to sell him, would you?'

Otto shook his head. 'We're very attached to him,' he replied.

When they had counted their takings, they found they had two hundred kobols – enough to pay the toll for each of them with eighty kobols left over.

'You see,' Juliet said to Maximillian. 'Cornelius

was quite right. We were meant to come on this adventure. Without us you wouldn't have even got inside the city.'

Slowly the queue shuffled forwards until at last the four companions found themselves passing through the great arched gates of the city. On either side stood two guards clutching long, wicked-looking spears. The one on the right was more or less like a man, except that his nose was extraordinarily bulbous and pitted, and his eyes were slightly too far apart. The one on the left had a long face like a wolf's, which ended in a snout and a mouth full of sharp yellow teeth. He stepped in front of them, raising his spear.

'What is your business in Abirkadash?' he demanded.

'We're sightseers from the north, come to admire the marvels of the city,' Maximillian told him, smiling broadly.

'The first guard turned to his companion. 'What do you think, Joot?' he asked.

Joot stared at them with his wide-set eyes, rubbed his bulbous nose and grunted. 'They're very ugly, Coot, but they look harmless enough.'

The first guard lowered his spear. 'All right, you can come in,' he said. 'That's a hundred and twenty kobols.'

Once inside the city, they found themselves in a cobbled square on which a number of stalls had been set up. Many of them were selling food, and pretty unpleasant looking food it was too. One stall seemed to specialise in bright red fungus that smelled like rotten meat. Another sold nothing but slabs of greyish blubber, and a third seemed to be doing a brisk trade in fat, white wriggling maggots.

'Come on,' Maximillian said. 'Let's get out of here before we're sick.'

He led the way down a narrow alley between two houses that leaned so closely together their roofs were almost touching. Down here, where the sun could not reach, it was already quite dark.

'I think we're going to have to find somewhere to stay the night,' Maximillian said.

'Will eighty kobols be enough for that?' Juliet asked.

Maximillian shook his head. 'Not a chance.'

'What are we going to do, then?'

'I think we may have to resort to a little bit of

magic. Have you got the rest of the money?'

Juliet handed over the cap with the remaining eighty kobols.

Maximillian looked quickly up and down the alley. When he was satisfied that there was no one in sight, he passed his hand back and forth over the cap, muttering to himself in the magical language he had used before. A moment later the hat was so full of kobols they were spilling over onto the ground.

Otto laughed. 'If you can pull off a trick like that, why bother having a job at all?' he asked.

'Because it doesn't last. These coins are only an illusion. They're not real, and whoever we give them to will find that out before very long. So we've only got a limited time to solve this case and get out of here.' He counted the money, gave a third to Otto and a third to Juliet, keeping the last third for himself. 'But remember, every transaction you get involved in increases the risk of discovery,' he warned them. 'So it's only for use in emergencies, or in case we get separated.'

Then he stuffed the cap back in his bag. 'Now then,' he said, 'let's see what sort of accommodation Abirkadash has to offer.'

They wandered about for some time through a maze of narrow streets littered with rubbish of every kind. Rats scurried in and out of the shadows, ignored by the elementals who went about their business, some on foot, some pushing handcarts, some on horseback. At last they came across a rather shabby looking two-storey house with a thatched roof and leaded windows. A sign above the door read, 'Molly's Boarding House'. Maximillian lifted the great iron knocker and the door was opened almost immediately by a middle-aged elemental woman in a floor-length multi-coloured patchwork dress. She was quite human-looking except for the size of her forehead, which was at least half as big again as a human's, and as smooth and shiny as an egg.

'Good evening,' Maximillian began. 'We were hoping we might be able to rent some rooms for a night or two.'

Molly surveyed the group and her eyes narrowed as she spotted Cornelius. 'As it happens, I do have three rooms vacant,' she told them, 'but I don't normally accept animals.'

'He won't be any trouble,' Juliet pleaded. 'He's ever so well trained.'

Cornelius made a low growling noise in his throat. Juliet quickly bent down and began stroking him.

'Well, I shall have to charge you extra,' the woman said. 'That'll be two hundred and fifty kobols, altogether.'

'It's a deal,' Maximillian told her.

She showed them upstairs to three tiny rooms, each about the size of a large cupboard. In each room there was a mattress on the floor along with a pillow and a couple of rather hairy blankets. That was the sum total of the furnishings.

'Ever so well trained, am I?' Cornelius said indignantly, once the woman had gone downstairs again.

'I'm sorry, Cornelius,' Juliet replied. 'I was only trying to keep that awful woman happy.'

'Huh!'

'If you ask me we've been ripped off,' Otto said. 'I bet elementals wouldn't pay two hundred and fifty kobols for these rooms.'

'Neither did we,' Maximillian pointed out. 'That money isn't real, remember.'

'Well that's just as well,' Otto said, because this place is a dump!'

No sooner were the words out of his mouth

than the most extraordinary thing happened. The floor seemed to ripple, as if a wave was passing through it. Otto, Juliet and Maximillian were thrown off their feet. Only Cornelius managed to stay upright.

'It's an earthquake!' Otto yelled.

'Let's get out of here, quick!' Juliet replied.

Maximillian got to his feet. 'Calm down everyone,' he said. 'It isn't an earthquake.'

'Then what is it?' Otto asked.

'Something I forgot to tell you about,' Maximillian replied. 'It's called the Domus.'

'What's that?'

'Tell me, have you ever heard someone describe a building as having a lot of character?' Maximillian continued.

'*I* have,' Juliet said. 'That's what my parents are always saying about our house. It may be cold and draughty but it has a tremendous amount of character.'

'Well in this world the buildings don't just have character, they have personality.' Maximillian continued. 'Most of the time that personality is dormant, but every now and again it wakes up. Especially if you say something uncomplimentary.'

'Wait a minute! Are you trying to tell me that I hurt this building's feelings?' Otto asked.

'Exactly!' Maximillian told him. 'So from now on, watch what you say. Now, I suggest we get some sleep. We've got a very busy day ahead of us tomorrow.'

They each took one of the rooms, Cornelius opting to sleep in Juliet's room. The mattresses were hard and lumpy and the blankets smelled musty, but they were so tired after walking for so long in the heat that they had no difficulty falling asleep.

In the middle of the night, Otto was disturbed by scratching noises coming from a corner of the room. He briefly considered getting out of bed to investigate but fell asleep again before he could make up his mind.

In the morning he woke up to find Maximillian standing over him. 'Come on, sleepyhead. We came here to find your mother, remember. Not for a holiday.'

Otto groaned and sat up. 'It wouldn't be much of a holiday,' he said. 'I don't suppose there's any chance of breakfast?'

Maximillian shook his head. 'I'm afraid the food in Quillipoth is pretty disgusting.'

'But we can't survive without eating!' Otto objected.

'I've got some sherbet lemons,' Maximillian replied. 'I've cast a hunger-suppressing spell on them.'

Once they were all assembled in Maximillian's room, he handed a sherbet lemon each to Otto and Juliet. 'I don't think they're really your sort of thing,' he told Cornelius, apologetically.

'That's all right,' the cat replied, sounding pleased with himself. 'I had three juicy, fat mice last night. This house is full of them.'

That must have been what I heard in my room last night, Otto concluded.

'Now then, if everyone's ready, I suggest we start our search for Otto's mother by visiting The Lushes,' Maximillian announced.

'What's that?'

'It's the part of town that respectable elementals avoid,' Maximillian told him. 'The part where the criminals hang out.'

'Is it safe?' Juliet asked.

Maximillian shook his head. 'It's very far from being safe, but it's necessary, I'm afraid. Anyone who doesn't want to come with me can stay here. No one would accuse you of cowardice, just common sense. So who's coming?'

'I am,' Otto, Juliet and Cornelius said, speaking simultaneously.

8

THE LUSHES

'Is there a government in Abirkadash?' Juliet asked as they made their way along a series of streets that grew progressively narrower, dirtier and more menacing.

'Certainly,' Maximillian replied. 'And a police force, too. But it's hopelessly corrupt. So most of the time it's a toss up to see who controls the city – the authorities or the criminals.'

They turned into a street lined with shops all selling what looked like piles of animal entrails heaped up in bowls.

'Is that what I think it is?' Otto asked.

Maximillian nodded. 'Entrails are something of a speciality in The Lushes,' he said. 'They call them Paunchy Pudding.'

Sure enough, in the window of one store a notice offered, *As much Paunchy Pudding as you can eat for forty kobols*.

'Do they cook them first?'

'I'm afraid not.'

'Ugh!'

'Honestly, you humans are so squeamish!' Cornelius said. 'There's nothing wrong with a bit of raw meat.'

'Corny! You're supposed to be a traditional cat, remember?' Juliet said, looking anxiously up and down the street. 'So if you could just restrict yourself to miaowing, we'd all be immensely grateful.'

'How boring you are!' Cornelius replied. 'Oh, very well,' he added as Juliet gave him her severest frown. 'I'll keep quiet – for now.'

Even without the shops selling entrails, it soon became clear that they had entered a part of Abirkadash with a very different atmosphere from the city centre. In the square near the great arched gateway where they had paid their toll, elementals hurried from place to place, intent on their business: lively, alert and voluble. But here it was a different story. The inhabitants of The Lushes leaned in doorways, sprawled on steps, or hung about in alleyways, staring glassily into space, or else regarding passers-by with curled lips and unfriendly expressions. The place felt like a powder keg waiting for a spark and Otto and Juliet glanced nervously about, feeling certain that their presence was far from welcome.

A sickly sweet odour hung in the air, beckoning to them from darkened doorways, wafting lazily from curtained windows, drifting down the street like a perfumed fog.

'What's that smell?' Otto asked.

'Ziffir,' Maximillian told him, 'or ziff for short. It's a drug made from the leaves of a plant that grows up in the mountains. Elementals smoke it because they believe it increases their magic powers. As far as I can tell, the only real effect it has is to make them more unpredictable and occasionally violent. So be very careful what you say or do.'

He had barely issued this warning when they heard a blood-curdling shriek and a tall thin elemental with a great mane of yellow hair came rushing towards them, brandishing an axe.

'Foreigners!' he yelled. 'Impostors!'

Terrified, they stopped in their tracks. 'He's going to kill us!' Juliet said.

Panic-stricken, Otto turned to Maximillian,

but the magical detective was already muttering to himself and making a series of rhythmic movements with his hands. A moment later, the charging elemental went crashing to the ground and lay there groaning pitifully.

'What did you do?' Otto whispered.

'Nothing serious,' Maximillian replied. 'I just cast a little spell to tie his shoelaces together. Come on, let's be on our way. We don't want to attract any more attention than we already have.'

They hurried down a side road, but already plenty of curious glances were turned in their direction.

'What was that all about?' Juliet asked.

'A few too many pipes of ziff, I should imagine,' Maximillian replied. 'And yet I doubt whether that's the whole story. Somehow or other, our friend with the hatchet must have sensed that we don't belong here. I suppose his magical senses must have warned him. And if *he* can work it out, so can someone else. Which means that sooner or later we're likely to get found out.'

'What can we do about it?' Otto asked.

Maximillian shrugged. 'Not very much, I'm afraid.' He reached into his pocket and brought out the rather battered paper bag of sherbet lemons. 'Here, have another sweet,' he suggested.

As Maximillian was handing round the lemon sherbets, Otto noticed a more than usually decrepit building a few doors down. In peeling blue paint, a sign above the door read, 'Urt's All Night Bar'. He pointed it out.

'What a stroke of luck!' the magical detective exclaimed. 'I believe this is the very place we're looking for. Come on everyone, let's go inside.'

Urt's bar was dark and gloomy and the air was thick with smoke. A few solitary customers sat at low tables, huddled over their drinks. All of them were smoking long black ziff pipes. Behind the bar stood a fat, bald human-like elemental with lank greasy hair and a large hairy wart in the middle of his forehead. He was dressed in a stained vest and baggy trousers and regarded the newcomers with an unfriendly expression. On the counter in front of him a glass of purple liquid steamed gently.

'Hello, Urt,' Maximillian said, sitting down on a bar stool. The others followed suit, even Cornelius jumped up on a stool and peered curiously at the proprietor.

Urt looked edgily at the newcomers. 'What do you want?' he said in a voice that sounded as if he was suffering from the worst cold in the history of medicine.

'Information,' Maximillian replied.

Urt sniffed so loudly that it made Otto jump. 'What sort of information?' he demanded.

'Yesterday someone kidnapped a female human from a bookstore on the other side,' Maximillian replied. 'We think they brought her here. Got any idea who might have done it?'

Urt spread his hands wide in a gesture that seemed to suggest he was only an honest hard-working elemental who couldn't possibly know about such things.'

'We're willing to pay good money,' Maximillian told him.

'Money doesn't interest me,' Urt said. 'You know that.'

'So what does interest you?'

Urt stared at Maximillian for a long time, then at each of the others in turn. Otto found it to be a distinctly unpleasant experience, as if he were being fingered by unseen hands.

Finally, Urt gave another vigorous sniff that turned into a grunt. Then he swallowed a few times, his Adam's apple bobbing about furiously, and pointed at Otto's sweater. 'How about your friend's sweater?' he said.

'This was a birthday present from my mother,' Otto protested.

A deeply unpleasant smile crept over Urt's face. 'I thought I sensed something special about it. They say a mother's love is a very powerful force. Now's my chance to find out. So what about it: my information for your sweater. Is it a deal?'

Otto hesitated. Even if he agreed to hand over the sweater, could they be sure that Urt would tell the truth? On the other hand they had no leads and they badly needed a break. So he had no choice, really. Reluctantly, he nodded his head and began to take off his sweater.

Maximillian stopped him. 'First the information; then the payment,' he said. He turned back to Urt. 'Well, do you know something, or don't you?'

Urt leaned more closely towards them. 'About a week ago I was talking to a couple of other Gallivants,' he said. 'People call them the Lily White Boys. Big chaps with blond hair. Not afraid of anyone. One of them was telling me they'd been offered a job with real money. So I said, what kind of job? Something that needed muscle, he told me. Someone on the other side had to be persuaded to come away with them.'

'Did he tell you who the job was for?'

Urt shook his head. 'Dried up altogether after that. Reckoned he'd said too much already.'

Maximillian nodded. 'Where can we get hold of these Lily White Boys?' he asked.

'You can usually find them at the Theatre Of Cruelty,' Urt told him. 'They do a bit of training there, I'm told.'

'OK,' Maximillian said. He turned to Otto. 'Give him what he wants.'

Otto took off the sweater and handed it over.

Urt accepted it greedily, holding it against his cheek and sniffing excitedly. This was too much for Otto. He looked away in disgust.

'Aren't you and your companions going to stop for a drink?' Urt asked when he had stowed the sweater under the counter. Now that he had got what he wanted, he seemed to relax and became almost eager to please. 'I've got the best fermented maggot juice you'll find anywhere in The Lushes,' he went on.

Maximillian shook his head. 'Thank you Urt,

but I think we'll leave the maggot juice for another day. Come on everyone.'

As they stood up to go, Otto's eye was caught by a strange contraption in one corner of the bar. It was made of brass and wood and looked like a telescope on a stand. On the wall beside it was written:

> Find out the truth
> Learn What Others Are Hiding From You
> Consult the Kryptoscope
> Only 10 Robols.

'How does that machine work?' he asked.

'Surely you've heard of a kryptoscope?' Urt replied.

Otto shook his head.

'Well my friend, your education has been sadly neglected,' Urt told him, rubbing his hands together gleefully. 'It's quite simple. You put a coin in the slot, put your eye to the lens and the kryptoscope shows you the secrets that others have been keeping from you.'

Otto turned eagerly to Maximillian. 'We can find out what's happened to my mother,' he said.

Maximillian shook his head. 'I wish it were

that simple, Otto,' he said. 'But you can't trust something like that. It will show you what it wants you to see, and I guarantee you no good will come from it.'

'Dear, dear, dear!' Urt said. 'Listen to old misery-guts! Let the boy have a look. It's just a bit of harmless fun, that's all.' He sniffed, swallowed and scratched beneath his armpit. 'Take no notice of him,' he told Otto. 'He just doesn't like to see people enjoying themselves. After all, what have you got to lose?'

'He's got a great deal to lose, thank you very much,' Maximillian said before Otto could reply. 'And now I think it's time we were on our way.' He took Otto by the arm and steered him quickly out of the bar.

Outside in the street, Otto turned stubbornly back towards the kryptoscope. 'I think it was worth a try, at least,' he said.

'Never trust a spell you haven't cast yourself, unless you know the spell-caster has your best interests at heart. Rule number one of *The Guide To Magical Investigation.*'

'And who wrote that?' Otto asked, crossly.

'I did.'

'I might have known!'

'I *do* know what I'm talking about, Otto. I understand how anxious you are to find out what's happened to your mother, but magic isn't something you can just tinker with. It's dangerous stuff. You saw what happened earlier with the axe-man. One mistake here and we could all end up dead.'

'Yes, but that machine shows you the things that are hidden from you,' Otto pointed out.

'So Urt claims. Look, you came to see me in the first place because you needed advice. And now I'm giving it to you. Stay away from the kryptoscope. OK?'

Otto grudgingly nodded, but for the first time since the two of them had shaken hands in Maximillian's consulting room he found himself resenting the magical detective.

'He just doesn't like someone else coming up with a good idea, Otto said to himself. 'He has to be in charge all the time, so he can have all the glory when the case is solved. Well, we'll see about that.'

9

THE THEATRE OF CRUELTY

'The Theatre of Cruelty is in the centre of the city,' Maximillian told them. 'So we'll need to take a cab.'

He led them to a main road where a variety of horse-drawn contraptions rattled past in both directions. Some were no more than plain wooden boxes on wheels pulled by a single half-starved animal; other carriages were elaborate and stylish, decorated with gold leaf or jewels and drawn by teams of plumed horses.

After a few minutes, they succeeded in flagging down one of the plainer vehicles, driven by a female elemental no bigger than Juliet. She had large pointed ears and wore a red riding habit with a pointed cap, which made her look a little like a miniature Santa Claus.

'Can you take us to the Theatre of Cruelty?' Maximillian asked.

'Course I can, guv'nor,' she replied in

a surprisingly deep voice, 'but you won't find nothing on at the moment. Though I do hear there's some lovely beheadings this evening.'

'That's all right,' Maximillian said. 'We just want to have a look around.'

They climbed inside the carriage and the driver set off. It wasn't a tremendously comfortable ride, for the streets of Abirkadash were cobbled and the carriage only had wooden wheels. More than once the passengers were nearly shaken out of their seats. Occasionally there were near misses with other vehicles; there seemed to be no rules governing the way the traffic behaved.

'What's the Theatre of Cruelty like?' Juliet asked.

'It's a huge open air arena where elementals fight each other, usually to the death,' Maximillian told her. 'They also stage public executions, floggings, torturings and various other kinds of punishment. A little while ago there was a rebellion. Soldiers loyal to an elemental called Crom fought government troops. Crom lost and hundreds of his men were taken to the Theatre of Cruelty to be put to death in front of a paying audience.

Apparently it took nearly a week to get through them all.'

'What did they do to Crom?'

'Oddly enough, nothing. He made a bargain with the authorities, you see. He agreed to surrender as long as he was allowed to go free. They allowed him to go free as long as they could slaughter his army.'

'He sounds like a pretty treacherous individual. Why did anyone ever follow him in the first place?'

Maximillian shrugged. 'Elementals are hard to understand. The one thing they respect above all else is power.'

Otto had remained silent throughout this conversation. The image of the kryptoscope was still fixed in his mind and he was firmly convinced that it could have provided the answer to all his questions if only he had been allowed to use it. But as they drew near to the centre of the city and the buildings became grander, he began to pay attention to his surroundings.

On their left a wide avenue of pillars led to an enormous mansion constructed of white marble. On the top, a great golden dome reflected the orange rays of the setting sun.

'What's that building?' he asked.

'That's Crom's palace,' Maximillian replied. 'They say a thousand elementals were worked to death building it. It was one of the very first buildings to be erected in Abirkadash and it's still one of the grandest.'

'Isn't this a very old city then?'

'Oh yes. It's thousands of years old.'

'I thought Crom was the one who started the rebellion?'

'He was.'

'But you said that wasn't very long ago. Yet the palace is thousands of years old. That doesn't make sense.'

'I forgot to mention that elementals live for an extremely long time,' Maximillian told him. 'They can be killed. Indeed, they kill each other all the time. But they don't normally die of natural causes. Nor do you see very many elemental children. They do have children, but only very rarely.'

'Why is that?' Juliet asked.

'Because elementals are incapable of loving, or even just liking one another. Most of them are far too interested in themselves.'

'I'm surprised the authorities still let Crom

live in such a grand building,' Otto said. 'Aren't they worried he'll start another rebellion one day?'

'I think they're frightened of him,' Maximillian replied. 'Crom is a lord, you see. That makes him a very, very important individual. Only elementals with a high level of magical ability are entitled to call themselves lords. Theoretically, he has to do what the government says but in reality he does whatever he likes.'

A few minutes later the cab drew up outside the Theatre of Cruelty and they all got out. 'Take my advice guv'nor,' the cab-driver said as Maximillian handed over the fare, 'come back for the executions tonight. There's at least a dozen and they'll make a first class show of it. You won't find a better night's entertainment anywhere around here.'

'We'll bear it in mind,' Maximillian replied.

The Theatre of Cruelty was an enormous circular building six storeys high. It was built with great stone blocks and was open to the sky. At regular intervals, there were vast arched doorways with numbers carved above them. It reminded Otto of pictures he had seen of the Coliseum in Rome, except that the Coliseum was a ruin, and this was a fully operational stadium. Despite the cab-driver's assurance that there was nothing happening this morning, there seemed to be plenty of people about, hurrying like ants in all directions.

Maximillian stopped one of them, a moon-faced individual with arms that reached down to his knees. 'Do you know where I can find the Lily White Boys?' he asked.

'They'll be in the training area. Go through arch number eleven and turn left. You can't miss it.'

'Thanks.'

'We'll have to handle this very carefully,' Maximillian said as they walked round the perimeter of the building looking for arch number eleven. 'We can't just walk up to them and ask if they kidnapped a woman from a bookshop.'

'So what *do* we say?' Otto asked.

'I'll go by myself,' Maximillian replied. 'I'll tell them that I've got a message from their boss and that he wants to see them.'

'But you don't know who their boss is,' Juliet pointed out.

'You know that, and so do I, but they don't,'

Maximillian replied. 'All I have to do is sound convincing enough and hope they don't ask too many awkward questions. Then we wait until they leave the building and follow them. The chances are, they'll lead us straight to the centre of this little conspiracy.'

'It's too risky,' Cornelius said.

'Shh!' said Juliet. She looked round quickly but there was no one within earshot. 'What do you suggest then?'

'If they see you, you're in trouble,' the cat went on, 'but they won't suspect me. Once Maximillian has spoken to them, you go back to the boarding house and I'll follow them.'

'Are you sure you'll be able to find your way back afterwards?' Juliet asked.

'Oh, please!' Cornelius said, indignantly. 'I'm not a human, remember. Cats have a built-in sense of direction.'

'It's a good plan,' Maximillian said as they drew level with arch number eleven. 'OK. The rest of you wait here. I'll go and talk to them.'

Otto, Juliet and Cornelius drew back into the shadows, as Maximillian walked through the archway, turned left and disappeared along a dimly lit corridor.

'I hope he knows what he's doing,' Juliet observed, 'because if anything happens to him, we're all in trouble.'

In fact, although Maximillian had seemed confident enough when he left them, he was by no means sure what he was going to say or do. Still, this was not an unusual situation for him. A detective must always be ready for the unknown, he reminded himself as he emerged in a large underground chamber.

In the middle of the chamber two elementals with long snouts and pointed teeth were engaged in armed combat. One wielded a sword, the other a spiked ball and chain. They circled each other warily, one lunging while the other dodged. The arm of the one with the ball and chain was badly cut and the ground was slippery with blood.

Watching this confrontation and offering occasional shouts of encouragement or jeers of derision, were two tall, muscle-bound elementals with short blond hair. They were identical twins, though one had a scar on his forehead. Apart from that they were impossible to tell apart. Both were entirely human-looking and dressed as they were in green T-shirts and tracksuit trousers, they would not have looked out of place in any gym or health club anywhere on Earth. Indeed, Maximillian suspected that this was where they had bought their clothes and possibly even got their haircuts.

At exactly the same moment they both looked up, saw the magical detective and began walking towards him. Both faces wore the same look of barely controlled violence, like a lion that has been disturbed while devouring its prey.

'Can we help you?' they asked, speaking simultaneously. Despite their apparent politeness, they sounded distinctly sinister.

'I've brought you a message,' Maximillian said. 'The boss wants to see you.'

'Now what could he possibly mean by that?' asked the twin with the scar.

'I really couldn't say,' the other one replied.

They both turned back to Maximillian. 'You'll have to be more specific,' they said.

'You know perfectly well what I mean,' Maximillian told them. 'There's a problem with the human you snatched. The boss wants to see you right away. You know where.'

They each raised an eyebrow. 'And who might you be?' the twin with the scar demanded.

'Just a messenger,' Maximillian replied.

'We've never seen you before,' the other twin pointed out.

Maximillian shrugged. 'Maybe you'll be seeing more of me in the future,' he said, turning to walk away.

The twin with the scar put his hand on Maximillian's shoulder and stopped him. 'We don't like to be messed about,' he said. 'I hope you understand that – for your own sake.' He squeezed the magical detective's shoulder so hard that Maximillian had to make a real effort not to cry out.

'No one likes to be messed about,' he said, removing the hand from his shoulder. 'And that includes me.' Then he walked calmly away without looking back.

The others were waiting anxiously outside. 'Did it go all right?' Otto asked.

'I think so. We'll soon see, anyway. Now we'd better get out of here and leave the next part of the job to Cornelius.'

Juliet crouched down beside the cat and

stroked him gently. 'Be careful, Corny,' she said.

For a moment Cornelius forgot himself. He rubbed his head against her leg and purred, just like any other cat. Then, remembering his dignity, he turned and walked away, sitting down in a shadowy corner where he was virtually invisible. Hastily, Otto, Juliet and Maximillian said goodbye and set off in search of a cab to take them back to their accommodation.

Cornelius did not have long to wait. No sooner had the others disappeared, than the Lily White Boys emerged from archway number eleven. They walked confidently, swaggering down the middle of the road, elbowing aside anyone who chanced to get in their way. As Cornelius followed at a respectable distance, a flaw in the plan occurred to him. What if the Lily White Boys decided to get in a cab? He would have to jump on the back and cling on, out of sight, while the carriage rattled furiously across the cobbles. It would be terribly dangerous and he might be spotted; but he would deal with that problem if it arose. He was a hunter, he reminded himself – stalking prey was in his blood and for the first time since arriving in this world, he was really beginning to enjoy himself.

In fact, the Lily White Boys showed no sign of summoning transport. Instead, they walked briskly through the centre of the city, stopping only once to aim a couple of vicious kicks at a beggar who was sitting by the side of the road. It soon became clear that they were heading for the palace of Crom.

'Well, well, well,' Cornelius thought to himself. 'So Otto's mother's kidnapper is one of the most powerful elementals in Abirkadash. I wonder what Max—'

But he never reached the end of that thought, for the world went suddenly black and he found himself being tossed this way and that. It took him a moment or two to realise that he had been put in a sack, thrown over someone's shoulder and was being carried away.

An image flashed into his mind – a shop window piled high with meat. 'Entrails are something of a speciality in The Lushes,' Maximillian had said. 'They call them Paunchy Pudding.'

Cornelius remembered the mice he had devoured the night before, how they had fled across the room, desperate to escape his clutches. But he had shown them no mercy. Was he now about to meet the same fate?

10

BAST

Being stuffed into a sack and carried over someone's shoulder is not very good for a cat's dignity. So when the mouth of the sack was finally opened, Cornelius looked a very sorry specimen indeed. His coat was ruffled, his eyes were staring, and he hissed and growled furiously, trying to slash with his claws at the hand clamped firmly around his neck. But it was no use. His captor knew exactly what he was doing.

'Naughty, naughty pusskins.' It was the voice of someone deeply unpleasant who was doing his best to sound nice. Cornelius was not taken in. He struggled and wriggled, trying to get a proper look at his captor, but succeeded only in catching a glimpse of two small horns and a goatee beard before the grip on his neck was released and he was dropped unceremoniously into a wooden box. The lid was slammed down on top of him and though he pushed against it with all his might, it would not budge.

Cornelius was now able to get a proper look at his captor through the wire mesh at the front of the box. Why did he recognise the face that grinned in at him so eagerly? Of course! This was the elemental who had offered to buy him when he, Juliet and Otto had stood outside the city gates and sung to those who were waiting to gain entry.

'Now then, pusskins,' the grinning elemental declared. 'You and I are going to become friends and you're going to earn me a great deal of money.'

That's what you think! Corny thought to himself. He was tempted to utter this sentiment out loud but he knew that if his captor found out he could talk it would only increase his value and lessen his chances of escape. So he contented himself with staring coldly back at the goat-faced elemental.

'I'll tell you what,' the elemental went on. 'I'll sing a few verses of one of my favourite songs and we'll see if you can join in.'

He opened his mouth and in an utterly tuneless voice began to sing:

I'm a very fine fellow,
With horns upon my head.
When my enemies see me,
They simply drop down dead.

There was a great deal more but it was all pretty similar and Cornelius soon stopped listening. When the goat-faced elemental finally stopped singing he regarded Cornelius with a disappointed expression. 'If you're not going to sing, you're no use to me,' he said. 'In which case, I'm going have to drown you. Think about that pusskins.'

With these encouraging words he walked out of the room.

While Cornelius sat inside the box, trying to think of a plan, Juliet gazed anxiously out of the window of Molly's Boarding House and sighed. The sun was sinking below the skyline and Abirkadash was growing darker by the minute. 'Surely he should be back by now?' she said for the umpteenth time.

'We don't know how far he had to follow the Lily White Boys,' Maximillian pointed out. They were all gathered in his room and he was sitting on the mattress with his hands clasped together, almost as if he were praying. 'Staring out of the window won't bring him back any quicker, Juliet.'

'I've had enough of this. I'm going to bed,' Otto said, getting up from the corner where he had been sitting with his head in his hands.

'Good idea,' Maximillian agreed. 'We should all do the same. We will need our strength tomorrow.'

Otto opened the door and was startled to find their landlady outside, in the process of straightening up, very much as if she had been listening at the keyhole.

'Oh…er…good evening sir,' she said. 'I was just coming up to see if there was anything else you might be wanting.'

'We'd just like to be left alone, thank you,' Otto said, giving her a hard look.

'Of course. I'll bid you good night then.'

Otto stayed exactly where he was until she had disappeared downstairs. Then he turned back to his companions. 'Do you think she was listening?' he said.

Maximillian shrugged. 'She wouldn't have heard much if she was. I shouldn't worry about it. She's just a nosy old woman.'

Otto nodded and went to his room, still fully dressed, he lay down on the bed and closed his eyes. Immediately, the image of the kryptoscope entered his mind. He could see it as clearly as if it were there in the room. If we had only used it, he told himself, we might not be waiting anxiously for the return of Cornelius. I might even be talking to my mother right now.

The more he thought about it, the more he resented the magical detective. Maximillian likes to pretend he has all the answers, Otto said to himself. But he doesn't really. Yes, he can do a few tricks, like multiplying money, but his magic has its limitations. It didn't work on the dog in the timber yard and so far it hasn't brought us any nearer to finding my mother. But if I had only looked in the kryptoscope I might have seen where she's being held! What harm could it have done?

Of course it was too late now. Or was it? Suddenly he remembered the sign above the door. In peeling blue paint it had read 'Urt's All-Night Bar'. All-night!

*

While Otto was thinking about this, no more than half-a-mile away in his wooden prison Cornelius was trying to remember something his mother had once said. She had been a wild cat and so had his father. Indeed, Cornelius was the first of his line for many generations to enter a human house. But he'd had no alternative; his mother had been killed by a motor car when he was only a kitten. He'd been close to starvation when Juliet found him.

No, he didn't regret his decision to become a domestic animal. But his mother would not have approved. She had no time for humans. 'Remember, we are of the line of Bast,' she had told him. 'She does not forget her children and we should never forget her.'

What else had his mother said about Bast? Cornelius struggled to remember and slowly her words came back to him. Bast was the first cat. No one knew where she came from, only that she appeared in our world many thousands of years ago, ready to produce her first litter. She was magical by nature and no enemy could ever defeat her. She lived nine times nine years and then one day she was gone. But before she disappeared, she promised that she would come to the aid of any of her children who called upon her in the hour of their greatest need.

Surely this was the hour of Cornelius' greatest need? Very well then. He would call upon Bast and see if she would answer him.

Most human beings have only two states of consciousness: they can either be awake or asleep. But for cats, there is always a third option. Cats call it 'stilling'. If you should see a cat staring into space without blinking for five or ten minutes at a time, then the chances are that cat is stilling. It's a state that is hard for humans to appreciate. They can be calm and quiet but, even so, their minds are usually busy remembering things that they have said or done, stories they've heard, sights they've seen. But when a cat stills, all thought disappears from its mind. It does not become vacant or stupid like a drunk or a drug addict; on the contrary, it remains highly alert and watchful, but there are no thoughts in its mind, only a great stillness as wide and deep as an ocean.

It was into this state that Cornelius now prepared to enter, but before he did so he focused his mind on one final thought: *Oh Bast, mother of all cats*, he begged, *come to my aid for I need you now as I have never needed you before.*

With that he began to still and the world around him faded away. He was no longer in the box, no longer in the home of the goat-faced elemental, no longer anywhere that we would recognise as a place. He had entered cat-space. And immediately he knew that he was not alone. Before him stood the most beautiful cat he had ever seen. Black as midnight, her coat like silk, her tail thick and lustrous, and her eyes as green as emeralds. She regarded him sternly.

'Ashtu-Pashtee,' she said.

This was his true name, the name his mother had whispered in his ear when he was first born. But he had not heard it for so many years, and he had begun to forget it himself.

'Bast,' he replied, 'thank you for answering my prayer.'

'I was tempted to ignore you, Ashtu-Pashtee,' she replied. 'Very tempted indeed. Do you know why?'

'No.'

'Because you have been a proud, lazy, ungrateful animal. That is why. You have sought the protection of humankind and forgotten what it is like to be cold, hungry and alone. You have turned your back upon the wild but you have not even been grateful for what you have received as a tame cat. Is it not so?'

Cornelius lowered his head. 'Yes, Bast. I'm sorry.'

'Very well. You are forgiven and I shall help you out of your present difficulty. But you must help yourself also, for I cannot burst open the box in which your body is trapped any more than you can. Instead, we must use a little cat magic.'

'Cat magic?' Cornelius said. 'But I don't know any.'

'If your mother had lived longer, she might have taught you some,' Bast told him. 'But that was my doing. It was I who called her back, for she had important work to do elsewhere. So now I shall teach you myself.' She stepped forward, touched his nose with hers and instantly he knew exactly what he had to do.

When the goat-faced elemental returned a few moments later, he crouched down in front of the box and regarded Cornelius with the same self-satisfied expression.

'Well, pusskins,' he said. 'Thought any more about what I told you?'

Cornelius stared back at him. But this was not just any stare. This was the magical stare that Bast had taught him. Within seconds, the goat-faced elemental was completely mesmerised. He could not move a muscle without permission from the owner of that gaze.

'In a moment, when I tell you to, you will open the lid of this box,' Cornelius declared. 'As soon as you have done that, you will open the front door of your house. You will stand aside while I leave and you will make no attempt to prevent me from doing so. Afterwards, you will forget everything that has happened. You will not recall seeing me, catching me in a sack or putting me in the box. There will be absolutely no memory of a talking cat. Is that all perfectly clear?'

'Yes, master,' the goat-faced elemental replied.

'Good. Then you may begin.'

The goat-faced elemental opened the lid of the box and Cornelius sprang out. Then he walked calmly over to the door that had now been opened for him. He hesitated in the doorway and looked up at the goat-faced elemental, who waited meekly for any further orders.

'One last thing,' Cornelius told him.

'Yes, master?'

'You will never, ever call a cat "pusskins" again. What will you never do?'

'Call a cat pusskins, master.'

'Good.' And with that, Cornelius walked out of the front door and set off to find his way back to Molly's Boarding House.

11

THE KRYPTOSCOPE

Otto waited a couple of hours until he felt sure that both Maximillian and Juliet were asleep. Then he opened the door of his room and, after checking that Molly was nowhere to be seen, tiptoed down the stairs and let himself out through the front door.

It was much darker than he had expected; there were no street lamps and what light showed in the houses nearby seemed to be produced by nothing more powerful than candles. It occurred to him that it might be harder to find his way to Urt's bar than he had expected. He glanced back at the boarding house and, for a moment, almost considered giving up the idea and going back to his room. But he reminded himself that the kryptoscope could hold the key to finding his mother. 'You can do it, Otto,' he muttered. 'Think of the surprise Maximillian will get when he finds you've solved the case all by yourself!' This cheered him up immensely and he set off for the bar without further delay.

If Otto had hesitated for just a few minutes longer he would have seen a carriage pulled by a team of coal-black horses come thundering out of the darkness and rattle to a halt beside Molly's Boarding House. He would have witnessed six burly elementals clambering out and knocking loudly on the front door. He would have seen that same front door opened almost immediately by Molly herself, who exchanged no more than a few words with the elementals before they entered the premises and went straight upstairs.

But he saw none of this. So there was no one to shout a warning as the door to Juliet's room burst open. She was lying on the bed, half dozing, when she suddenly found herself confronted by three savage-looking elementals with long snouts and sharp teeth. They were dressed in black tunics and three-cornered hats. One held up a lantern and the other two brandished swords.

'Police!' said the one with the lantern. 'You're

under arrest on suspicion of passing counterfeit money. On your feet!'

Terrified, Juliet did exactly as she was told.

'Now put your hands out in front of you where we can see them. And before you or your friend in the next room try any tricks, I should warn you that we took the precaution of setting up a magical damping field before we left the station. So any spell you or your friend attempt to cast will be automatically neutralised. And the spell will follow you both around. Understood?'

Juliet nodded. Meekly, she put out her hands and one of the elementals tied them tightly together. Then she was pushed out of the room and down the stairs where the landlady stood, shaking her head disapprovingly. No doubt it was she who had contacted the police, Juliet thought to herself.

Once out in the street, Juliet was ushered into a waiting carriage where she found Maximillian already sitting between two more police officers. He too had his hands tied together but he did his best to smile encouragingly. 'Don't worry,' he told her. 'It will be all right.'

'No talking!' one of his escorts ordered sternly.

When they had all squeezed inside, one of the elementals leaned out of the window and shouted for the driver to set off. A moment later they were rushing headlong through the unlit streets. Juliet could not imagine how the driver managed to see where he was going, for outside there was nothing but inky blackness.

Throughout the journey, Juliet kept thinking about the Theatre of Cruelty and the dreadful events that took place there. Was that where she would end up? Would she and Maximillian provide the next evening's entertainment for a bloodthirsty audience?

At last they arrived at the police station, where they were marched to separate cells and locked up. Juliet's cell was entirely bare, without even a bench to sit on. High up in the rear wall was a tiny barred window. Other than that there was nothing but brick walls and a heavy wooden door. But at least her hands had been untied. She sat with her back against the wall and shut her eyes, her mind filled with unanswerable questions. What was going to happen to her now? Was there even the slightest hope of rescue? Where was Otto? Why had he not been captured? And what had happened to Cornelius? It was all so confusing.

As a matter of fact, Cornelius was almost as bewildered as Juliet. A little earlier he had left the house of the goat-faced elemental and tried to work out the way back to Molly's Boarding House. It wasn't easy, despite what he'd said earlier about cats having a built-in sense of direction. He'd been taken to the elemental's house in a sack so there were no familiar sights to use as landmarks. Nor could he rely entirely on his nose. A cat's sense of smell is fourteen times more powerful than a human being's but everything in Quillipoth smelled strange and unidentifiable. He cast around desperately for a familiar scent, but it was the equivalent of a human being standing in the middle of an amusement park on a busy Saturday in the middle of the Summer holidays, trying to listen for a friend calling out his name half a mile away. After a while, Cornelius realised that the only thing he could rely on was his instinct. So, concentrating as hard as he could, he summoned up a mental picture of the boarding house and tried to let it draw him in the right direction.

He saw all kinds of sights as he roamed the city. There were beauty parlours where elementals had their ears or their noses tattooed, their feathers combed or their scales polished. There were market stalls that sold nothing but jugs of warm blood, others that offered bones for their customers to gnaw on, and everywhere there was paunchy pudding. There were shops full of swords, daggers, cutlasses, scimitars, crossbows, axes and maces. And a whole boutique devoted exclusively to tail jewellery. He was sorely tempted to stop and look at this more closely but he knew he needed to get back to the others. Besides, his earlier experience in the sack had made him much more wary.

Eventually, he found himself in familiar territory, and before long he was turning into the road in which Molly's Boarding House was situated. That was when he saw Otto coming out of the front door.

Cornelius was just about to run towards him when he realised that there was something slightly odd about the way Otto was behaving.

Sneaky, that was the word for it. Otto was darting from doorway to doorway like…well, very much like Cornelius himself might do if he had just stolen a piece of fish from Miss Honoria Belsham's kitchen. Clearly he wanted to stay hidden, but from who? And exactly *where* was he going?

Hidden in the shadows, Cornelius watched as Otto turned the corner. Should he go after him? Or should he find the others and ask them what was going on? The question was answered a moment later when a carriage appeared out of the darkness and drew up outside the boarding house. Half a dozen uniformed elementals disembarked and hurried inside the house. It was obvious they were police officers and therefore that there was trouble of some kind. Cornelius decided to forget about Otto until he had found out what was going on. Within minutes the elementals had re-emerged, with Maximillian and Juliet. Both had their hands tied.

Now Cornelius was thoroughly frightened. He had to run after Otto and tell him about the police raid. Of course by now Otto had disappeared from sight, but it wasn't too difficult to discover where he had gone. He knew Otto's smell well enough (a mixture of books, biscuits, toothpaste, sherbet lemons, and the usual odour of young human). He could also hear Otto's distinctive footsteps echoing in the deserted streets up ahead.

As Cornelius gained on Otto, he slowly realised where the boy was heading. Urt's All-night Bar! What did this mean? Was he planning some secret deal with Urt? Was he responsible for informing the police about his friends? Surely not! But if not, then what was he up to?

A moment earlier it had been Cornelius' intention to catch up with Otto and tell him what was happening. Now he was not so sure. He decided that he should follow Otto and find out exactly what was going on before making himself known. So he remained out of sight and observed Otto came to a halt outside Urt's bar. For a moment the boy paused, as if unsure about the wisdom of what he was doing. Then, making up his mind, he opened the door and went inside. Cornelius tried to dart in after him but he was too late. The door closed and he was left out in the street.

*

Urt's bar looked exactly the same as it had during Otto's first visit – the same solitary customers were slumped over rickety stained tables, smoking their pipes of ziff. The same sickly smell hung in the air – a mixture of the drug, ancient sweat and some kind of alcohol, probably the fermented maggot juice that Urt had boasted about. Urt himself was standing behind the bar just as before, except that this time he was wearing Otto's sweater. It was much too small for him but he didn't seem to care.

'Well, well, well! If it isn't my little friend from the other side,' Urt said with a grimace that he no doubt intended as a smile. 'What can I do for you?'

'I want to have a look in the kryptoscope,' Otto replied.

'Of course you do,' Urt said. 'Never mind what old misery-guts tells you, eh? You can make your mind up for yourself.'

Otto ignored this. He wasn't going to get drawn into a conversation with Urt. 'How much does it cost?' he demanded.

'Just ten kobols. You've got to admit that's

good value,' Urt said, holding out his hand.

Briefly, Otto recalled Maximillian's warning about using the magical money, and he felt distinctly uneasy. But then he told himself that it was he and Juliet who had earned the money, with the help of Cornelius. Otto certainly didn't remember hearing Maximillian sing. The way he saw it, that meant he had every right to spend it on the kryptoscope if he wanted to. Having successfully disposed of his conscience, he put his hand in his pocket, took out the money and handed it over.

Urt pressed a button behind the bar and the room was filled with a low humming noise. 'The kryptoscope is at your disposal,' he announced.

Now that the moment had finally arrived, Otto felt surprisingly nervous. Nevertheless, he took a deep breath, bent over the machine and put his eye to the lens.

At first he could see nothing at all but a kind of swirling blackness and he was just about to complain when something began to take shape. He was looking at a house, a very big house, and one that was vaguely familiar, though he could not place it for some reason. As the picture came more clearly into focus he realised that the house was on fire, or at least a part of it was.

The picture changed and he saw a man in middle age standing in the middle of a book-lined room. This must have been a picture from the past, for the man's bushy side-whiskers, his clothes and the furniture in the room all suggested an earlier era. The man was unlocking a drawer in a desk and now he took something quite small out of the drawer and held it up.

Otto found that if he concentrated hard enough on any detail, that part of the picture became larger, as if a camera were zooming in closer. So he concentrated on the thing that the man had taken out of the desk and saw that it was a coin or a medal of some sort. Holding the coin at arm's length, the man spoke some words in a foreign language. He repeated the same phrase very slowly and deliberately several times, as if he were trying to remember it. Bell-ee-jah kee-pah-tam. 'Bell-ee-jah kee-pah-tam.'

Suddenly the expression on the man's face changed. He seemed to be staring fixedly at the far corner of the room with naked fear in his eyes. Otto focused his attention in the same direction and the object of the man's terrified gaze became clear.

Low down, close to the floor in the corner of the room, a pool of shadow had begun to form. As Otto watched, it grew taller, and there was movement within its midst. Soon it had grown into a pillar of seething darkness about the height of a man. The more closely Otto looked, the more distinctly he could see the shapes that moved within that darkness, and the more terrified he became. There were eyes that stared back at him and they were full of anger. Hands tried to claw their way out of the darkness. Mouths opened to let out silent screams of pain. It was as if dozens of people had been imprisoned within a pillar of black smoke.

Otto struggled to look away from this horrible monstrosity but he found he could not turn his head. Instead, he felt himself being sucked further in, so that he seemed to be standing right beside it. And now the pillar began to change once more. It grew arms and legs and a head until it was recognisably human in form, though still a writhing mass of disembodied shapes.

'I don't want to look!' Otto cried.

But he had no choice.

A hole opened in the creature's head where a mouth might have been, and out of that hole came a voice that chilled Otto's blood.

'You have summoned me.'

'I haven't summoned you!' Otto shouted. 'I don't know who you are and I don't want to know. Get away from me!'

Just when he thought he could stand it no longer, the kryptoscope went dark and Otto found himself released from its spell.

He straightened up and found that his legs were trembling and his body was bathed in sweat.

Urt grinned at him from behind the counter. 'What's the matter?' he asked with a sneer. 'Didn't you see what you were expecting?'

'No I didn't,' Otto told him. 'I don't know what that was all about but it was nothing to do with me.'

'What a shame! You know I hate to see a dissatisfied customer.'

It was so obvious he didn't mean this that Otto decided not to waste any more words on this ugly elemental. He turned to leave.

And that was when he saw them.

Two elementals were standing with their backs against the door and their arms folded. They both had blond hair and were identical in appearance except that one had a scar on his forehead. They looked as if they could have picked Otto up and torn him into little pieces without breaking into a sweat.

'You're coming with us,' they told him, stepping towards him and seizing him by the arms.

'Ow! You're hurting me!' he objected, for they had gripped him so hard he felt as if his bones might break.

'We like hurting people,' said the one with the scar.

'It's our hobby,' the other one added.

With that, they led him out of the café and into a waiting carriage.

'Where are you taking me?' Otto demanded as the carriage began careering through the narrow streets of The Lushes.

They refused to answer his questions. There was nothing he could do but regret his foolishness in setting off for Urt's bar without telling the others. Now they wouldn't even know where to start looking for him.

Although it was dark outside, Otto had no difficulty recognising their destination when the carriage finally came to a halt. Crom's palace was illuminated by a light that had no obvious source, but which Otto suspected was magical in origin.

The Lily White Boys hustled him out of the carriage and around the side of the building, entering through an unobtrusive doorway. As soon as he stepped inside the palace, Otto was met by an overpowering sense of dread that grew in intensity as they hurried him along endless shadowy corridors. He felt as if he were being led through a labyrinth, at the centre of which some hideous beast was waiting to devour him.

When they finally stopped outside a pair of enormous wooden doors studded with huge iron nails, Otto knew without the slightest doubt that whatever he feared lurked within.

One of the Lily White Boys knocked on the door and a voice called for him to enter.

To Otto's horror, it was the voice from the kryptoscope, the voice that had come from the writhing pillar of darkness.

The Lily White Boys opened the doors and pushed Otto forwards. He found himself in a vast chamber, as big as a cathedral. Most of the room was empty but at the far end, seated on a golden throne, was a hooded figure dressed all in grey with a painted white mask for a face. Otto had no doubt that this was Crom, who had worked a thousand of his fellow elementals to death to build his palace and who had bargained away the lives of thousands more when his rebellion had been unsuccessful.

'You may approach me,' Crom said. His voice was not loud, yet somehow it carried easily across the great space that separated him from Otto.

A roll of carpet the colour of blood stretched from the throne all the way to where Otto now stood. Despite the trembling in his legs, Otto began to make his way along it.

Once, when Otto had been about eight-years-old, he had found the body of a dead bird in the yard at the back of the bookshop. Curious about the processes of death, he had got a stick and turned the carcass over, only to find that it was full of maggots. He could still remember the mixture of disgust and horror that had filled him at the sight. It was the same feeling that seized his whole body now as he stood before the throne and forced himself to look directly at the creature seated upon it.

'Well?' Crom said. 'Have you got it?'

Otto's mouth felt as if it were filled with dust and his tongue seemed to be stuck to the roof of his mouth. 'I don't know what you mean,' he managed to say.

'You cannot hide anything from me,' Crom told him.

'I'm not trying to hide anything,' Otto replied.

'We shall see.'

A moment later, Otto knew that in some way his mind was being searched. It felt as if a knife were slicing mercilessly through his brain; he cried out. Finally it stopped.

'You miserable fool!' Crom said contemptuously. 'You understand nothing. I should turn you to dust right now.'

Otto had no idea what Crom had expected him to bring. Or why he had expected him to bring it. Nor was he particularly interested in finding out. There was only one question that mattered to him. 'What has happened to my mother?' he demanded.

To his surprise, a low mocking laugh issued from behind the painted mask.

'Tell me where she is,' Otto cried.

The laughter ceased. 'Your mother is dead,' Crom told him.

12

TRIAL BY FIRE

When Juliet awoke, she was still sitting in the corner of the cell and she was very stiff and cold. By the meagre light filtering through the barred window, she could tell that it was morning outside, but she had no idea whether it was early or late. She got to her feet and walked around the cell, rubbing her hands together to warm herself. The circulation had just returned to her fingers and toes when the cell door opened and two of the snout-faced police officers entered the room.

They ordered her to take off her shoes and socks. Then she was led outside to where Maximillian stood surrounded by several more police officers.

The sight of the magical detective, who had seemed so powerful when she first met him, standing barefoot and surrounded by guards made her heart sink. He looked rather depressed but he did his best to smile in Juliet's direction. The magical damping field that her captors had warned her against had obviously taken away his powers.

The pair of them were marched along a corridor, up a flight of stairs and along another corridor until finally they emerged in a courtyard open to the sky. Juliet felt a wave of heat engulf her.

Sitting on a raised platform at one end of the courtyard was a very important-looking elemental. He was immensely fat and completely bald, with large, bloodshot eyes and jowls that would not have disgraced a bloodhound. He wore a purple robe and a black cap. Juliet suspected that he was a judge of some sort.

On all four sides of the courtyard, elementals of all kinds were sitting on benches and talking animatedly amongst themselves. But Juliet scarcely noticed them. Her attention was fixed on the shallow rectangular pit in the centre of the courtyard. The air above it shimmered in the heat and as Juliet looked more closely, she realised that the pit was filled with red-hot coals. 'They're going to burn us to death!' she thought to herself. If she had been frightened before, she was now utterly terrified and her whole body shook.

When he caught sight of the prisoners standing in the doorway, the judge made a sign. Two very short elementals in red and yellow tunics who stood on either side of him raised trumpets to their lips and produced a harsh, tuneless blast of sound. Immediately the buzz of conversation ceased.

Juliet and Maximillian were dragged forward to jeers and hisses from the crowd.

'Let the charges be read,' the judge continued.

A tall thin elemental with bright yellow feathers on her head rose up from one of the benches and, holding up a piece of paper, read aloud in a high-pitched voice, 'The defendants are charged with knowingly using counterfeit money to pay for goods and services.'

Upon hearing this, the hostile noises from the crowd increased in volume.

The judge raised his hand for silence then turned to Juliet and Maximillian. 'This is a matter of the utmost seriousness. As every citizen of Abirkadash knows, the penalty laid down by the law for such a crime is death.

However, in keeping with the custom of the city you will have a chance to prove your innocence in the usual fashion.'

'What is the usual fashion?' Juliet asked, though she was so frightened her voice was barely audible.

'You must walk barefoot across the bed of red-hot coals,' the judge informed her. 'If you are innocent, you will not be harmed. If, however, you are guilty…' He did not bother to complete his sentence because it was perfectly obvious what would happen.

'That's ridiculous!' Juliet said. 'It won't prove whether I'm innocent or not. I won't do it!'

'Let me undergo the trial on behalf of both of us,' Maximillian volunteered.

But the judge shook his head. 'You will each take your turn, beginning with the girl. Now, let the trial begin!'

'This isn't fair!' Juliet cried, her eyes beginning to fill with tears. 'I don't even belong here.'

The spectators seated around the sides of the courtyard were leaning forward in their seats, eager to see her step into the pit. They began to chant, 'Burn! Burn! Burn!' At the same time the guards began pushing and pulling her forwards. 'Somebody help me, please!' Juliet yelled.

Suddenly there was a blinding flash of light and when Juliet opened her eyes, the courtyard was full of green smoke. All around her people were shouting in confusion.

She guessed that this was Maximillian's doing. Somehow he must have managed to regain a little of his magic powers. Now was her chance to escape! But first she had to shake off the guards, and to her dismay, no matter how she struggled they clung on determinedly.

By now the judge had begun making himself heard over the babble of confused voices. 'Remove this smoke at once!' he demanded

The smoke cleared as quickly as it had appeared but almost immediately it was replaced by a feeling of fear and dread that seemed to fill the courtyard. It was so strong that Juliet felt as if she might be physically sick, and it was clear from the expressions on the faces of her guards and of the spectators that everyone was experiencing the very same thing. Even the judge had turned pale. He was staring in the direction of the doorway through which Juliet and Maximillian had entered just a few minutes before.

A tall figure in a long grey robe was standing there. He wore a hood over his head and his face was covered by a painted white mask. There was no doubt that it was he who was responsible for the terror that now gripped everyone.

'My Lord Crom!' said the judge. He sounded unsure of himself. 'To what do we owe the honour of this visit?'

Crom turned his head and seemed to gaze for a moment directly at Juliet and Maximillian. 'There will be no further need for this trial,' he said. His voice was as cold as snow on a tombstone in the depths of winter.

'No need for the trial?' the judge replied. 'But why, my lord?'

'Because I take responsibility for the prisoners,' Crom replied. 'They are not from this world and I have decided that they are to be returned to their own world without delay.'

'And on whose authority do you assume this responsibility?' the judge demanded.

'On my own responsibility.'

The judge hesitated. Finally, rather grudgingly,

he said, 'Well, this is most irregular. However, under the circumstances I believe that the court can accommodate your lordship's wishes. It is the sentence of this court, therefore, that the prisoners be banished to their own world never again to return. I will make arrangements for the banishing to be carried out and in the meantime...'

'Enough!' Crom interrupted. 'I will carry out the banishing myself.'

'My lord Crom, it would be better if this were done in the proper manner,' the judge replied.

'Are you questioning my judgement?' Crom demanded. He did not raise his voice but the level of fear in the courtyard rose palpably higher.

'I would not dream of doing so, my lord.'

'I am pleased to hear it. You may all leave now, except for the prisoners.'

'Leave, my lord?' The judge looked as if he could hardly believe his ears. 'But this is the House of Correction. I am the presiding judge. Surely you mean that you wish to have the prisoners removed to an appropriate location, in which case I can arrange for a suitable escort?'

'I mean what I say,' Crom continued. He raised his voice for the first time and the judge looked as if he had been struck in the face. 'Get out of here immediately, all of you, unless you wish to earn my displeasure.'

The spectators wasted no time doing as they were told. The guards on either side of Juliet and Maximillian quickly joined the stampede to reach the exit. Crom stood aside and watched as they crowded past, not even daring to glance in his direction. The last to leave was the judge, who paused for a moment and looked directly at Crom. 'I shall have to make a full report of this matter,' he said.

'I do not think so,' Crom replied. He lifted one gloved hand and pointed at the judge who screamed. Then a crack appeared on his face, and another, and another, spreading over his whole body like a broken pane of glass. A few seconds later he crumbled into a little pile of dust.

The only people left in the courtyard now were Juliet and Maximillian. Crom turned to them and raised his right hand.

For a moment Juliet thought that he was going to turn them to dust too and she wondered how painful it would be.

But Crom had other plans. 'I am not someone who is accustomed to being disappointed,' he said. 'But you and your friend Otto have disappointed me greatly. Now go, and do not return without it!'

He seemed to draw a shape in the air with his hand and the next moment Juliet and Maximillian found themselves standing beside the fountain in the abandoned garden of Belsham Manor. There was no flash of light, no feeling of motion, no physical sensation whatsoever. One moment they were standing in the courtroom, the next they were not.

Juliet turned to Maximillian. 'What happened?' she asked. 'Did you have some sort of agreement with Crom all the time? And what did he mean: do not return without it? Without what?'

Maximillian shook his head. 'I've no idea,' he said. 'The flash of light and the green smoke were my doing. I was hoping it would create a diversion that would give us an opportunity to get away. But everything that happened after that is a mystery to me.'

'So what are we going to do?' Juliet asked.

'The others are still stuck back there. We have to go back and get them.'

'Of course we do,' Maximillian said. 'But first we need to try and understand what exactly is going on. Because at the moment we're simply stumbling around in the dark.'

After a moment Juliet said, 'Have you ever wondered what this Janusian Portal is doing here in the first place?'

'You know, I think that's a very good question,' Maximillian said. 'What *is* it doing here?'

'Maybe we should ask the owner?' Juliet suggested.

'Miss Honoria Belsham?'

'Yes.'

'Of course!' Maximillian said. 'You're absolutely right! What have I been thinking of? If you want to solve a mystery, you need to start at the beginning – not in the middle.'

'Well come on, then. What are we waiting for?' Juliet said.

And with that she began striding purposefully through the wilderness in the direction of Belsham Manor. A moment later, Maximillian followed.

13

THE ELEMENTARIUM

Miss Honoria Belsham was eighty-three years old. She looked as if you could have blown her over with one breath, but despite her frailty, a keen intelligence was at work behind those bright blue eyes. When Juliet knocked on the door of Belsham Manor, introduced her friend and explained that he was interested in the history of the house, Miss Honoria smiled and invited them into her sitting room.

Despite living so close by, Juliet had never before stepped inside Belsham Manor. She saw at once that the room into which Miss Honoria led them was absolutely full of priceless antiques. History seemed to hang in the air like smoke and Juliet would not have been surprised to find that she had gone back a hundred years.

Miss Honoria lowered herself cautiously into a wooden rocking chair and invited her two guests to seat themselves on a leather sofa. 'What would you like to know?' she asked.

'Anything you can tell us about the house,' Juliet replied.

Perhaps you could start with Sir Henry Belsham,' Maximillian suggested.

So Miss Honoria recounted the story that everyone who lived in Bridlington Chawley had heard many times before: how Sir Henry had been so successful in business that he had earned the nickname Lucky Henry, how he had decided to retire to Bridlington Chawley, built Belsham Manor and finally how his wife and new-born son had been killed in a fire. 'Despite his nickname, he was not a lucky man,' she concluded.

'I wonder, do you have any original documents from Sir Henry's time?' Juliet asked. 'Letters or a diary or anything like that?'

'There's not very much left, I'm afraid,' Miss Honoria said. 'I got rid of most of the old books a long time ago, sold them to the bookshop in the town. I was rather pressed for money at the time, you see. A house like this requires a great deal of keeping up and the bills can be very expensive.'

'Just a minute,' Maximillian said, sitting forward eagerly in his chair. 'Do you mean Spinoza's bookshop?'

'Yes.'

'And when was this?'

'Well I couldn't say exactly but it must have been about twelve years ago. Why do you ask?'

'Oh, I just wondered whether there would be any of those books left in the shop,' Maximillian replied airily, but Juliet got the feeling that this was not the whole truth. She suspected that a deeper motive lay behind his question and that in some complicated jigsaw puzzle within the magical detective's mind, pieces were beginning to fit together.

'So there's absolutely nothing left from Sir Henry's library now?' Juliet went on.

'I did find some papers in a wooden box in his study after I'd sent the rest to the bookshop,' Miss Honoria said. 'But they just seemed like notes for some research Sir Henry had been doing. He was very interested in antiquities, I believe.'

'Could we possibly have a look at them?' Juliet asked.

'I don't see why not,' Miss Honoria replied.

'I'll go and see if I can find the box.'

When Miss Honoria had left the room, Juliet turned to Maximillian. 'Why did you ask about the bookshop?' she whispered. 'Is it important?'

'It might be,' the magical detective whispered back. 'Otto's father died of some mysterious tropical disease about twelve years ago. The doctors thought he must have contracted it from an insect in a crate of books he purchased.'

'You think the insect might have been in a book he bought from Miss Honoria?'

'If it really was an insect that caused Mr Spinoza's death,' Maximillian said enigmatically.

Before Juliet could question him further, Miss Honoria came back into the room holding a small wooden box. 'This is it,' she said. 'Though I don't imagine you'll find it very enlightening. You'll have to treat the papers with a great deal of care because, like me, they're getting rather fragile.'

She handed the box to Juliet who opened it and took out a number of folded sheets of paper. She spread the separate pages out carefully and began to read. But the handwriting was very old-fashioned and some passages seemed to be in a foreign language. Baffled, she passed the papers to Maximillian, who studied them carefully. After a few minutes he looked up with an expression of shock on his face.

'Are you feeling all right Mr Hawksmoor?' Miss Honoria asked.

'Perfectly all right, thank you,' he replied. 'You say you read these pages, Miss Honoria? Do you have you any idea what they refer to?'

'Well, it's a bit hard to follow,' the old lady replied. 'I think there must be some pages missing. But it seems to be a description of an object Sir Henry was interested in, something called an Elementarium.'

Maximillian nodded. 'The Elementarium of Belshazzar,' he said. He carefully refolded the papers and put them back in the box. 'Do you know much about the early history of your family?' he asked.

'Nothing much before Sir Henry, I'm afraid' Miss Honoria told him. 'It's all a bit of a mystery. Though I do remember my mother once saying that she believed that the Belshams originated somewhere in the Middle East.'

'Really?' Maximillian said. 'That's very

interesting. Well it's been extremely interesting talking to you and we're very grateful for giving us your time.' He got to his feet.

Juliet could tell he had found out something important. He was doing his best not to show it but he was almost quivering with subdued excitement.

Miss Honoria rose from her chair to show them out. As they stood in the hallway saying goodbye, Juliet noticed a coat of arms on the wall.

'Is that the family crest?' she asked.

'Yes. Rather unusual, isn't it?' Miss Honoria replied.

It was unusual. Two lions stood on either side of a circular shield which was divided into four sections. Each section was occupied by a triangle, two with their pointed ends facing upwards and two with their pointed ends facing downwards. Two of the triangles had horizontal lines through them. Underneath was a scroll on which were written the words 'Belli Ja Kippatam'. Something about the design struck Juliet as very familiar.

'I'm afraid I've no idea what the motto means,' Miss Honoria said. 'I was never very good at Latin when I was at school.'

Maximillian frowned. 'It's not Latin,' he said after a moment. 'It's Akkadian, a language spoken in Ancient Babylon about three thousand years ago.'

'Good heavens!' Miss Honoria said. 'Do you know what it means?'

Maximillian nodded. 'It means, the master has arrived.'

'What a very strange motto,' Miss Honoria said. 'Are you sure that's right?'

'Quite sure,' Maximillian told her. 'Thank you so much for your help, Miss Honoria. It's been a most fascinating visit.'

The moment that Miss Honoria had closed the door behind them, Juliet remembered where she had seen the Belsham coat of arms before.

'Stay here!' she told Maximillian. 'I'll be back in a minute.'

She ran along the path that led from Belsham Manor to her house, let herself in through the front door and raced upstairs to her room. There it was on top of the chest of drawers – the coin her father had found when digging over Miss Honoria's flower beds. She picked it up and looked carefully at it. Yes, there was the same design of four triangles she had seen on the Belsham coat of arms. She ran back outside to where Maximillian stood waiting and showed him the disc.

'Good grief!' he exclaimed. 'How long have you had this?'

'About a week,' she replied. 'My father dug it up in Miss Honoria's garden. He thought it was a Roman coin.'

Maximillian shook his head. 'Unless I'm very much mistaken, this is the very thing that Sir Henry was so interested in.'

'The elementarium of Byzantium?'

'Yes.'

'And you think it's got something to do with Otto's mother's disappearance?'

'Yes I do. But I'd like to pay another visit to Spinoza's bookshop, just to clear up a few loose ends before I jump to too many conclusions. I'll explain about the elementarium on the way.'

He handed the metal disc back to Juliet who put it in her pocket. Then they set off down the hill.

'Well, let's start at the beginning,' he said. 'An elementarium is a magical object, fashioned by a human being in order to gain power over an elemental. The one that your father dug up in Miss Honoria's garden is the most famous of its kind. It was made over three thousand years ago for the Babylonian prince, Belshazzar, so that he could summon and bind to his service one of the most powerful elementals of all.'

'Crom?' Juliet suggested.

'Correct.'

'And did it work?'

'Oh yes, it worked extremely well. But Crom is a very proud individual and he hated running errands for Belshazzar. So while he faithfully carried out the orders he was given, he secretly worked on Belshazzar's mind until Belshazzar became convinced that there was a plot to assassinate him. One evening he became so frightened he ordered his guards to kill anyone who tried to enter the palace. But even this didn't make him feel better. He became sick with worry and decided to take a walk in the fresh air to clear his head. He slipped out by a back door and walked about for some time, thinking the same anxious thoughts over and over again. At last he decided to return to the palace, but by that time he had forgotten the orders he had given earlier. He walked straight through the front door and was killed by his own guards.'

What happened to the elementarium after that?' Juliet asked.

'It disappeared. There were various stories about it popping up in different parts of the world. Whether or not they were true is anybody's guess, but all agreed on one point. Whoever possessed the elementarium always came to a very unpleasant end.'

'Wait a minute!' Juliet said. 'If the elementarium gives the user power to command Crom, why can't we use it to order him to find Otto's mother?'

'Because it only works for the rightful owner,' Maximillian told her, 'which means someone directly descended from Belshazaar himself.'

'Is that why you asked Miss Honoria about the history of her family?'

'Exactly. And, if you recall, she said the Belshams originated in the Middle East, which is where the ancient kingdom of Babylon was located.'

'OK,' Juliet said, 'that bit makes sense. But

I still don't understand where Otto and his mother fit into all this.'

'That's what I'm hoping our visit to the bookshop will make clear,' Maximillian replied.

But when they got to the bottom of the hill they realised they had forgotten one thing: Spinoza's bookshop was closed.

'We'll have to break in,' Maximillian declared.

'What if the neighbours hear us and call the police?' Juliet objected.

'That's a chance we'll have to take. Come on!'

They made their way round to the back of the building and used a rubbish bin to clamber over a wall into the yard.

Maximillian was just looking around for something to help him break a window when Juliet discovered that the back door was unlocked.

'That's a stroke of luck!' she said. 'Otto must have forgotten to lock it when he was looking for his mother.'

Once they were inside, they quickly made their way to the apartment upstairs.

'What are we looking for?' Juliet asked, as Maximillian began opening drawers and rifling through their contents.

'Anything that doesn't seem right,' the magical detective replied. 'I know that's not very helpful but it's the best I can do. We're just going to have to rely on hunchability.'

'I'm not sure how hunchability works, exactly.' Juliet objected.

'Don't worry, that's exactly how it should be,' Maximillian assured her. 'The more uncertain you are, the greater your powers of hunchability are likely to be.'

The two of them worked their way systematically through every drawer, cupboard and filing cabinet in the apartment. Juliet was on the point of giving up altogether when she came across a cardboard folder with the words 'Family Documents' written on the front. It contained a lot of certificates, medical records and such like, but at the very bottom was an unmarked brown envelope. She opened it carefully. Inside was a piece of burnt cloth about three inches square. As soon as she looked at it, she found herself tingling all over as though an electrical current had passed through her body. This must be what hunchability feels like, she said to herself, excitedly.

She showed the folder and the piece of cloth to Maximillian.

'Now that's interesting,' he said. 'Very interesting indeed. 'Tell me, is Otto's birth certificate in that folder?'

'It doesn't seem to be,' Juliet replied. 'Both his parents' birth certificates are here but there's no sign of Otto's.'

'Just as I thought!' Maximillian said.

'What do you mean?'

Well I may be wrong, of course,' the magical detective replied, 'but it suggests to me that Mr and Mrs Spinoza are not Otto's parents at all.'

'You mean he was adopted?'

Maximillian shook his head. 'If that were the case, there would be correspondence from the adoption agency. No, I think our friend Otto was stolen.'

'Stolen!'

'Yes, but for the very best of reasons.'

'I don't understand,' Juliet protested.

'There isn't time to explain properly,' Maximillian told her. 'We need to get back to the Janusian Portal as soon as possible. Come on!'

'Wait!' Juliet said. 'We can't go back to

170

Quillipoth that way. Don't you see? It's exactly what Crom wants us to do. "Do not return without it," he said. He must have meant the elementarium. He didn't really mean to banish us at all. That was just for the benefit of the court. He wants us to come back with the elementarium and he'll be waiting on the other side to take it from us.'

'Of course!' Maximillian. 'You're absolutely right. You know, you're really getting the hang of hunchability now.'

'That wasn't hunchability,' Juliet said, scornfully. 'It was just common sense.'

'There must be a way round this,' the magical detective said, ignoring Juliet's remark. He thumped the flat of his hand against the side of his head. 'Think, Hawksmoor, think!'

'I don't suppose you could use this, could you?' Juliet said, putting her hand in her pocket and bringing out the elementarium. 'You did say it was a very powerful magical object.'

Maximillian looked doubtful. 'Well, I suppose it's theoretically possible,' he said. 'But it would be like, I don't know, trying to use somebody else's computer account without their password.'

'But people *do* use other people's computer

accounts without their passwords,' Juliet pointed out. 'Hackers do it all the time. Couldn't you do a bit of magical hacking?'

Maximillian looked thoughtful. 'I suppose I could try,' he agreed. 'The thing is, how to do it without alerting Crom. Wait a minute! Yes, it might just work!' He suddenly sounded tremendously excited. 'Have a look around the apartment and see if you can find me some salt and a mirror – a small one will do. Oh, and some black cloth.'

Juliet found a bag of salt in the kitchen, a small make-up mirror and a black velvet jacket in Otto's mother's bedroom. She brought them to Maximillian who was busy clearing a space in the middle of the sitting room.

He looked at the black velvet jacket and shook his head. 'That's much too big! Fetch me a pair of scissors!'

'You can't start cutting up Otto's mother's clothes,' Juliet objected.

'This isn't a question of fashion,' Maximillian replied. 'If Crom learns what we're up to none of us, including Otto's mother, will ever need to worry about wearing a jacket again.'

By the time Juliet had returned with a pair

of scissors, Maximillian had moved all the furniture to the edges of the room, taken up the rug and was busy creating a large circle on the floor with salt. When he had finished this task he took the scissors and cut a small square out of the back of Mrs Spinoza's jacket.

'Now all we need are some candles,' the magical detective continued. 'We may have to buy those. Otto told me that his mother wouldn't have them in the house. Apparently she was terrified of setting the house on fire. I should have put two and two together when I heard that, of course, but I didn't.'

'I don't know what you're talking about,' Juliet told him.

'No, no, I don't suppose you do,' Maximillian replied. 'Never mind. All will become clear in due course.' He took some money out of his pocket and handed it to her. One of the shops nearby must sell candles,' he said. 'Have a look, will you? Oh, and try not to get scented ones. They make me sneeze.'

With that he produced a piece of chalk from his pocket, knelt down on the ground and began drawing on the floor.

Juliet had to walk some way before she

found a shop selling candles, and by the time she got back to the apartment Maximillian had drawn all sorts of odd-looking shapes and characters upon the floor within the circle of salt. He took the candles, placed them at regular intervals around the perimeter of the circle and lit them.

'Now I can't guarantee this will work,' he told her, 'because I've never tried hacking into an elementarium before. But in principle I can't see why it shouldn't. The main thing is that we should both be standing within the circle, so if you could just step inside without disturbing the salt or any of the chalk marks.'

Juliet stepped cautiously into the circle.

'Thank you, that's fine. Now the problem we have to contend with is this: the elementarium was designed to summon Crom, a bit like a dog whistle summons a dog. So the moment I start activating it, Crom will be aware of what's going on. The elementarium will become a kind of third eye for him, through which he will be able to see everything that we are doing.'

'We can't let that happen!' Juliet protested.

'No, no, of course not. That's the point of the mirror and the cloth. I know it's not very sophisticated and it probably won't work for very long but it might just confuse him for long enough to enable us to cross to Quillipoth before he understands what I've done.'

'What *are* you going to do?'

'A little exercise in misdirection. The basis of all conjuring tricks. Watch! I place the cloth on the ground at the centre of the circle, like this. I draw another smaller circle of salt around it, like so. Then I place the elementarium on top of the cloth and put the mirror face down on top of the elementarium. Now when the elementarium is activated, all that Crom will see is a reflection of the elementarium itself floating in a black background. Of course he'll very quickly realise what's going on, but by then we should have been transported to his world and the magical charge should have evaporated.'

'And he won't be able to trace it?' Juliet asked.

'Well, I can't say that for certain,' Maximillian said. 'But this is the best I can do. Now I need you to close your eyes and think about the beach we arrived at when we crossed over for the first time. I should warn you, there may be a bit of a drop in temperature. And a few odd sensations. But it can't be helped. Are you ready?'

Juliet closed her eyes. 'I think so.'

'Right then. Here we go!'

14

INSIDE CROM'S PALACE

By coincidence, at exactly the same time that Juliet and Maximillian had been breaking into Spinoza's bookshop, Cornelius had been breaking into Crom's palace. Although, as Corny himself had pointed out earlier, where magic is concerned there is no such thing as coincidence.

After finding himself shut out of Urt's All Night Bar, Cornelius had no idea what to do next. However, while he was still debating the best course of action, he saw the Lily White Boys arrive at the bar. There was no chance of slipping in after them because they looked all round before entering, but he did not have long to wait before they exited again. To his horror he saw that Otto was sandwiched between them.

Cornelius watched as they bundled him into a carriage and set off. At the last minute, he managed to jump onto the back of the departing vehicle where he clung on for dear life. The journey that followed was extremely unpleasant and more than once he thought he would end up broken and bleeding on the cobbled street. But somehow he managed to keep his position until the carriage pulled up outside Crom's palace.

Greatly relieved, he jumped down and watched as Otto was taken inside. Cornelius knew he could not risk following the Lily White Boys too closely, so he made his way round the building looking for an alternative point of entry. At last he spotted an open window at the rear. It was on the first floor but, fortunately, there was a large tree nearby. It was only a matter of climbing up the trunk, walking along a branch and jumping down onto the windowsill. No great problem for an animal gifted with four sets of sharp claws and a superb sense of balance.

Once inside the building, he found himself in an extremely large and ostentatious bathroom. It seemed that elementals shared the bizarre human habit of immersing themselves completely in water. Cornelius shuddered at the thought. To his relief the door had been left ajar so he quickly stepped outside into a corridor.

Now that his magical senses had been sharpened, Cornelius was intensely aware of the personality of Crom's palace – what Maximillian had called its Domus – and he realised that it was also aware of him. It had been trained to recognise intruders and right now it was beginning to realise that something was very wrong. At any moment an alarm would sound and guards would come running from every direction.

Cornelius decided it was time to use some more of the magic Bast had shown him. He began to purr from the deepest part of his being, imagining that purr reaching out and filling the space around him. He visualised it moving through the air and entering the minds of all those it reached as if a swarm of bees were buzzing around inside their heads.

It was not long before he felt the bewilderment of the palace Domus, as it struggled to understand what was happening and to locate the source of the disturbance. When the purr was resonating strongly and continually, Cornelius went on his way once more and no alarm sounded. Gradually he felt the Domus relaxing its watchfulness and slipping back into its natural, dormant condition.

But there were still the palace guards to contend with. They were a bit more sophisticated than the Domus. The Deep Purr would merely bounce off them. Cornelius was still wondering how he should deal with the guards when he very nearly walked into two of them as he turned a corner. He was only saved by the fact that the guards were looking straight ahead, not at the floor. So he had just enough time to dart behind a vast stone urn.

As soon as they had gone past, he followed, keeping out of sight. After a while he heard one of them say, 'What did they do with the prisoner?'

'Locked him up in the cellar with the other one,' the second guard replied.

That was useful! Cornelius stopped following them and began looking for a way down. It didn't take him long to come upon an elaborate marble staircase. This was the most frightening part of the experience so far, for once he had ventured onto that staircase there was absolutely nowhere to hide. Luckily, he reached the bottom without encountering anyone and found himself in a grand hallway. Corridors led off in three different directions. He chose the one that looked the least grand. It led him to a much smaller set of steps going still further down into the depths of the building.

No sooner had he descended this second staircase than he began to pick up Otto's scent. It stood out quite clearly amid all the elemental smells.

It wasn't difficult to work out where the scent was coming from. At the bottom of the stairs an ape-like elemental stood on guard outside a door. Cornelius had no doubt Otto was imprisoned behind it.

'Halt!' the elemental shouted, brandishing a sword that was several times the size of Cornelius. 'What is your purpose here?'

Cornelius did the only thing he could think of. He rubbed his head against the elemental's leg and tried to look as soppy and friendly as he could. It wasn't magic but it had always worked in the past. And today was no exception. The ape-like elemental looked down at him with his sword still clutched in his hand and his mouth wide open. He sheathed his sword, crouched down and began to stroke Cornelius, making silly baby noises.

That was Cornelius's chance. He raised his head and looked straight into the elemental's eyes, using the stare that Bast had taught him. It meant he had to stop the Deep Purr. But what choice did he have? He focused all his concentration on the elemental's eyes.

'Listen very carefully,' he began.

Even as Cornelius was beginning the process of reaching into the guard's extremely sluggish mind, on the other side of the door Otto was pacing back and forth in a state of nervous agitation. Since he had first walked into this cell and found his mother sitting on a chair looking up at him with a mixture of delight and dismay, he had gone through just about every emotional response that was humanly possible.

He'd been overjoyed to find that his mother was not dead, despite what Crom had told him, and the two of them had spent quite a long time just hugging and saying how pleased they were to see each other. But, of course, Otto's mother was also very upset to find that her son had also been taken prisoner, and she insisted that he tell her in detail about how he had ended up in this position. That meant explaining about the magical detective agency and about finding the map in the *Guide To The World's Rarest Birds*.

At this point Otto had tried to get some of his own questions answered, like how his mother had known about the Janusian Portal, why she hadn't told him about it, and just who she had thought was going to find the map in the book. But she had been very reluctant to provide him with an explanation, assuring him that everything would be made clear in due course and insisting that he carry on with his own story.

So Otto told her about Urt's all-night bar and the kryptoscope. When he had got to the Lily White Boys she'd shuddered and said, 'I know all about them already. They were the ones who kidnapped me.'

'But I still don't understand why,' Otto said. 'What made them pick on you?'

Before Otto's mother could reply, the door to the cell opened and the guard stood in the doorway with Cornelius beside him.

'Oh no! Not you too, Corny,' Otto said.

But Cornelius ignored him. Instead he stared up at the guard and said, 'You will hand the key to the cell to the boy.'

To Otto's surprise, the guard did exactly as he was told.

'Now you will stand in the corner and do absolutely nothing while everybody else leaves the cell. Is that clear?'

'Yes, master,' the guard replied.

'Afterwards, you will remember nothing of this. What will you remember?'

'Nothing.'

Cornelius turned to the prisoners. Otto was grinning from ear to ear. His mother was sitting with her mouth open in astonishment as she tried to decide which was stranger: a talking cat or the guard's behaviour. 'No time for explanations,' Cornelius said. 'Just follow me.'

Once they were outside, Otto locked the cell door. 'I have no idea what you just did Corny, but it was a pretty smart trick,' he said.

He had hardly finished speaking when Cornelius felt the Domus wake up. A moment later alarm bells began to ring all over the palace.

'Which way do we go?' Otto asked.

'I don't know,' Cornelius said. He had been so busy thinking about freeing Otto and his mother from their cell that he hadn't considered how they might get out of the palace. He couldn't see them climbing out of the bathroom window and leaping onto the tree. But he was given no time to think of an alternative plan because at that moment a group of guards appeared at the other end of the corridor. 'This way!' he yelled and set off running in the opposite direction.

A moment later more guards appeared at the other end of the corridor. Cornelius, Otto and his mother screeched to a halt.

'In here!' Otto yelled, opening a door at random and darting inside.

The others followed and they found themselves in a narrow stairwell. 'We have to get to street level,' Cornelius said.

'Let's go then,' Otto said.

They ran up the stairs, two at a time. But there were far more stairs than they had expected and soon they were forced to slow down.

'Shouldn't we have reached the ground floor by now?' Otto's mother asked. She was looking very red in the face.

'I think we must be past the ground floor,' Otto said.

'Then why haven't we seen an exit?' Cornelius demanded.

'I don't know,' Otto replied, 'but I'm beginning to think we might have made a mistake choosing this staircase.'

On and on they went and still the stairs wound back and forth above their heads. They had slowed down to a walking pace by now but there didn't seem to be any sign of their pursuers.

'Perhaps they didn't see where we went,' Cornelius suggested hopefully.

'Or perhaps they know we're trapped,' Otto replied.

After that no one said very much. They saved their breath and concentrated on putting one foot in front of the other. At last they reached a final flight of steps. Ahead of them was a door.

'What if they're waiting for us behind that door?' Cornelius asked.

'Then we're caught,' Otto replied. 'But we can't stay here because we're too frightened to go any further, can we?' With that, he opened the door and stepped out to find himself gazing up at a thousand stars.

It took him a little while to realise that he was standing on the rim of the golden dome on top of Crom's palace. Below him the city of Abirkadash was spread out in all its glory. A narrow causeway led around the dome with a guard rail the only thing between Otto and a fall of hundreds of metres.

'It's all right,' he called back to the others. 'There's no one here. Come and look at the view.'

His mother and Cornelius stepped out to join him.

'That's all very well,' his mother said, 'but what are we going to do now?' Her habit of worrying was too deeply ingrained to be affected by an aerial view of the city, no matter how breathtaking.

'That staircase must lead here for a reason,' Otto suggested.

'Like what?' Cornelius asked.

'I don't know. We could try walking round the dome and seeing if there's another way down.'

'Whichever way we go down, they'll be waiting for us at the bottom,' his mother said gloomily, but she followed as Otto led the way around the great golden dome.

'That's odd,' Otto said, coming to a halt when he had completed only about a quarter of a circuit. 'Someone seems to have left a carpet here.'

Sure enough, on the causeway ahead of them was a richly patterned carpet. Even in the darkness, its deep colours seemed to glow like jewels.

'Why would anyone do that?' his mother asked.

Cornelius took a few steps forward and sniffed at it cautiously. 'It doesn't smell right,' he said. 'It isn't made of whatever carpets are usually made of.'

'What is it made of then?' Otto asked.

'I think it might be made of pure magic.'

'It's a trap! It has to be,' Otto's mother said.

'I'm not so sure,' Otto replied. 'Let's think about this. There's a staircase that leads nowhere else except here. There's a carpet that isn't really a carpet at all but is made of magic. What does that suggest to you?'

'Absolutely nothing,' his mother said.

'That's because you're not using hunchability,' Otto said. 'Let your mind relax. Try not to search for the solution. Let the solution come to you.'

'When I was a little girl,' Otto's mother said after a moment, 'My favourite stories were from the *Arabian Nights* and they were full of magicians who rode about on magic carpets.'

'Perhaps that's what this is,' Otto said excitedly. 'A magic carpet – Crom's emergency escape route in case all else fails.'

'So you think we should just get on it and let it whisk us away to who knows where?' Cornelius suggested.

Just then there was a shout. Looking up, they saw that the door at the top of the stairs had opened and a guard had emerged, followed by another, and another.

'I think that settles it,' Otto said. He stepped onto the carpet, followed quickly by his mother and Cornelius.

There was no doubt that they had come into contact with a powerful magic of some kind. Otto could feel a low vibration that seemed to enter his body and make it tingle all over. But the carpet did not move an inch.

'Someone needs to work out how to make this thing fly,' Cornelius said, 'and they need to do it fast!'

He was right. The three guards were working their way steadily around the dome. In another minute there would be no hope left.

'Try to think, Mum!' Otto urged, struggling to keep the panic out of his voice. 'What happened in those stories? How did they get the carpets to fly?'

'I don't know,' she said. 'I think they just thought of where they wanted to go and the carpets obeyed them.'

Otto closed his eyes and summoned up the long stretch of greenish sand, beside the slate-blue ocean where he had first entered Quillipoth.

Nothing seemed to happen

'We might as well surrender!' he said, despairingly. But when he opened his eyes he found the carpet floating gracefully through the starry sky and beneath them the golden dome of Crom's palace gradually disappearing into the distance.

15

THE MASTER

When Juliet had accidentally blundered into the Janusian Portal, the experience had been disturbing but not especially unpleasant – a bright flash of light and a sensation a bit like dropping very quickly in a lift. But hacking into the power of the elementarium was a very different matter. She felt as if her whole body was being liquefied and squirted at great speed through a nozzle. When she finally found herself standing on the beach, she was shivering with cold and ready to be sick.

'Sorry about that,' Maximillian said. He was looking a bit green himself. 'It didn't go very smoothly, did it?'

'Not very smoothly!' Juliet protested. 'I feel like I've been turned into a milkshake.'

'I must remember to include an anti-nausea spell if I ever have to do that again,' Maximillian said. 'Still, at least, we got here and there's no sign of Crom.'

'There's no sign of anything,' Juliet pointed out. 'It's pitch dark.'

'Your eyes will adjust in a minute,' Maximillian told her. 'There's quite a lot of light, actually. It's a full moon.'

Juliet looked up at the sky and immediately her attention was caught by something altogether more unexpected than a full moon. 'What's that?' she asked, pointing to the improbable silhouette gliding silently through the air in their direction.

'I don't know,' Maximillian said slowly. 'But it looks an awful lot like a woman, a boy and a cat sitting on a flying carpet.'

'That's what I thought,' Juliet agreed.

A few minutes later the carpet drifted gently down to earth a few yards away. Cornelius, Otto and his mother got to their feet and calmly strolled over to greet them.

'You've rescued your mother!' Maximillian exclaimed. 'This is remarkable! Well done, Otto!'

'It was Cornelius, actually,' Otto admitted. 'He rescued both of us.'

'Well done, Corny!' Juliet said. She bent

down and Cornelius allowed himself to be stroked for several seconds before finally walking away and washing his fur modestly.

'What happened to you?' Otto asked.

'We were arrested by the police and locked up,' Juliet told him.

'How did you manage to get away?'

'I set them free,' said a voice behind them and immediately all their joy at seeing each other drained away, to be replaced by cold terror. They turned to face Crom, hooded and dressed all in grey, except for the painted mask that hid his face.

'I think you know what I have come for,' he continued. 'Let's not waste any more time.'

Maximillian put his hand in his pocket and brought out the elementarium.

At this, a deep sigh came from behind Crom's mask. It was the sound of someone who has waited hundreds of years to achieve his ambition and who now has the thing he most desires within his grasp.

But Maximillian was not prepared to grant the elemental's wish so easily. He shook his head. 'It is not mine to give you, Crom. Nor is it yours to claim,' he said. Instead he held the metal disk out to Otto. 'Take it,' he said. 'It belonged to your father, though it did him no good in the end. Now it is your turn to be its master, and these are the words you must speak...'

But before he could finish the sentence, Crom lifted his hand and instantly, Maximillian froze, his mouth half open, his eyes full of dismay and despair.

'Do you imagine I have waited all this time to see a child lord it over me?' Crom asked. He turned to Otto. 'Your friends cannot help you now,' he said.

It was true. His mother, Juliet, Cornelius and Maximillian all stood as still as statues in a park. From the look in their eyes Otto could tell that they were fully aware of what was happening but unable to move a muscle.

'So it is just you and me,' Crom went on, drawing back his hood and removing his mask. Behind, there was nothing but a featureless darkness in the shape of a man's head. Darker than the night but alive with movement, as if it were seething and boiling beneath the surface. It was a sight that turned Otto's blood to ice, but was also somehow familiar. Where had he seen it before? It was so hard to think properly with

Crom's implacable will bearing down upon him.

'Give me the elementarium!' Crom ordered.

The urge to reach forward and hand over the metal disk was almost overwhelming. Almost, but not quite. Somehow Otto found the strength to resist.

'If you will not give it to me, then I will have to take it myself,' Crom said, his voice full of anger. He rushed forward and his hands closed like a vice around Otto's neck.

Otto fought as hard as he could but Crom was much bigger and stronger than he was. 'I'm going to die,' he thought to himself as he kicked out helplessly. Suddenly he remembered what Maximillian had said about hunchability. 'It means using your imagination and following wherever it leads.'

As Crom's hands tightened around his throat, Otto tried to let his mind go blank, to surrender entirely to his imagination.

Into his mind rushed the picture he had seen in the kryptoscope. A man dressed in old-fashioned clothes holding up a small metal disk just like the one that Maximillian had given him and speaking in a foreign language.

What was it the man had said? Otto

focused on the picture and again he heard those alien-sounding syllables. Somehow he summoned up the strength to join in. His lips shaped the words and in the faintest of whispers he muttered, 'Bell-ee-jah kee-pah-tam.'

Instantly, Crom's grip loosened. He stepped backwards and bowed his head. 'What would you have me do?' he asked, his voice flat and expressionless once more.

Otto took a few moments to recover himself. He did not fully understand what had happened, only that his hunch had proved correct. It appeared that Crom was now completely within his power! 'Release my mother and my friends from your spell,' he ordered, hope filling him.

Crom made a gesture with his hand. In an instant the paralysis that had gripped the others vanished. Maximillian grinned broadly at him. Juliet made a thumb-up sign.

'Now you will promise never, ever to trouble any one of us again, directly or indirectly,' Otto continued. 'Is that clear?'

'Yes.'

'If you disobey me or break this promise in any way, I will order you to destroy yourself,' Otto continued.

He had no idea whether he really had such a power but it was clear that Crom believed he did, for he bowed his head and said, 'I will not disobey.'

Otto turned to Maximillian. 'Can you send us back or should I ask Crom to do it?'

'I think I can manage,' the magical detective replied.

'Then go back to your palace and stay there until we've left your world,' Otto told Crom.

The elemental bowed once more.

A moment later he was gone.

Everyone immediately began talking at once, congratulating Otto, wanting to know how he had done it and how he had known what to say until Cornelius finally said, very loudly and firmly, 'I think I've had enough of this world now. Can't we go back home and sort out all the explanations there?'

'Quite right,' Maximillian said. 'Fortunately, I took the precaution of bringing one or two necessary items with me.' From his bulging pockets he produced a bag of salt, four candles and a box of matches. 'I think we can dispense with the mirror and the black cloth this time. Oh yes,' he added, glancing at Otto's mother.

'I'm afraid I have a confession to make about a jacket of yours.'

'Let's not bother about that now,' she told him. 'I just want to get home.'

'Of course,' he agreed, beginning to mark out a large circle with the salt.

'Remember the anti-nausea spell, this time,' Juliet told him. 'And an anti-turning-people-into-milkshake spell, if you know one.'

'Don't worry, it's all under control,' Maximillian replied. Now if everybody would just stand in the circle, and if I could just borrow the elementarium for a moment, Otto.'

Otto handed it over.

'Everybody close your eyes and think of Spinoza's Second-hand Bookshop,' Maximillian ordered.

And they did.

16

THE HEIR TO BELSHAM MANOR

'I still don't understand everything that's happened,' Otto said. 'What has the elementarium got to do with me? Who was the man I saw in old-fashioned clothes? And why did Crom kidnap my mother in the first place?'

They were in the sitting room above the shop drinking mugs of tea and making short work of a packet of chocolate biscuits, all except Cornelius who was enjoying a large bowl of full cream milk. Since returning to Earth, he had been behaving much more like an ordinary cat, but there was no doubt that the magic had affected him permanently because he could still talk. (Or, as he might have put it, the others could still understand him.)

Maximillian turned to Otto's mother. 'Do you want to explain it all, or shall I?' he asked.

'I'd much prefer it if you did,' she said.

'Very well,' the magical detective said. 'But it's a long story and I'm not sure I know all the details. It starts over three thousand years ago when the Babylonian prince, Belshazzar, had the elementarium made by his magicians so that he could become the most powerful man in the world. It gave him the power to command Crom. But Crom is a treacherous individual and Belshazzar came to a sticky end. After that, the elementarium disappeared for a very long time until it ended up in the possession of Sir Henry Belsham, who must have been a direct descendant of Belshazzar since the elementarium can only be controlled by a family member.'

'Was he the man I saw in the kryptoscope?' Otto asked.

'Undoubtedly.'

'And Crom became Sir Henry's servant?'

'Yes. He had no alternative. The master of the elementarium is Crom's master, too. Crom is forced to carry out his wishes and forbidden to harm him. Those are the rules that govern the elementarium.'

'But Crom found a way to break the rules and harm Sir Henry?'

'Yes he did. Unfortunately, this is where my

explanation becomes no more than guesswork but I imagine that once Sir Henry had made his fortune, he found that it wasn't enough. He wanted an heir, someone who would carry on the family name. So he got himself a bride. Whether this was the result of magic or natural human affection I can't say but when she told him that she was going to have a baby, he must have felt that he had achieved all his heart desired.

'But Sir Henry's joy was Crom's misfortune, for now there was yet another generation to whom the elementarium could be passed on. Crom decided to act.'

'The fire!' Otto said.

'Exactly. Crom caused the fire which killed Sir Henry and his wife.'

'And his baby,' Juliet pointed out.

Maximillian shook his head. 'Not the baby,' he said.

'So what happened to the baby?' Otto asked.

'Let's just focus on the day of the fire for a moment,' Maximillian said. 'It took place on the very same day that Sir Henry's son was born. Now it's my belief that with the birth of his heir, Sir Henry decided that he was finished with the elementarium. After all, he had achieved everything he desired and now he wanted to be rid of Crom. But he couldn't bring himself to destroy the thing completely, just in case he ever needed it again some day. So he decided to bury it in the garden, under one of the flagstones beside the fountain. After recording this decision in his diary, he went out to the garden, lifted the stone and hid the elementarium beneath it. He'd just replaced the stone when he saw smoke coming from the house.

'Now, let's leave Sir Henry there for a moment and come back to the present. Well, not quite the present, actually. Twelve years ago to be precise.' He turned to Mrs Spinoza. 'Perhaps you'd like to tell the next part,' he suggested.

Otto's mother sighed. 'If I must. Well, as you know, my husband bought the contents of Sir Henry's library from Miss Honoria. Among the books, he found the diary in which Sir Henry described hiding the elementarium. That was Sir Henry's own map that you found in the bird book. Of course, as soon as he had read about the elementarium, he decided to look for it.

I can still remember that day as if it was yesterday. He went off late in the evening by himself and when he came back he had a baby boy with him. I asked him where the child had come from but all he would tell me was that he'd saved the boy's life and we mustn't tell anyone about it because they wouldn't understand and they'd take him away. It was only much later that I learned the whole story. Anyway, I expect you can guess what happened next. We called the baby Otto and brought him up as if he was our own.'

'Then I'm really Sir Henry's son?' Otto said in amazement. 'But that doesn't make sense. Sir Henry lived a hundred and fifty years ago!'

'I think what must have happened is this,' Maximillian replied. 'When Sir Henry noticed the smoke coming from the house he suffered a terrible shock. That shock must have worked on the elementarium. It's a very powerful object, after all, and quite capable of transporting people back and forth in time as well as across worlds. So when Mr Spinoza picked it up a hundred and fifty years later, that great rush of emotional energy drew him back to Sir Henry's time. He immediately saw what was happening and rushed into the house along with Sir Henry. Perhaps Sir Henry tried to rescue his wife while Mr Spinoza grabbed the newly born child. But only one man came out of the burning building alive. Mr Spinoza. Still clutching the baby, he went back to the fountain where the magic of the elementarium was still active and he was returned to his own time.'

'So if Otto is Sir Henry's son, that makes him the real owner of Belsham Manor, doesn't it?' Juliet said.

'Yes, it does. But I think that might be a bit difficult to prove in a court of law,' Maximillian said with a smile.

'Then what happened to my father?' Otto asked, 'My stepfather, I suppose I should say. That tropical disease he died of, was it real?'

Mrs Spinoza shook her head. 'I've never understood that,' she said.

'Well I think we can make a reasonable guess,' Maximillian said. 'I imagine that when Crom learned that his plan to destroy the last of Belshazzar's descendants had been thwarted, he placed a curse on the man responsible for spoiling his scheme, and that was what killed him.'

'So that was why Crom said that my mother

was dead,' Otto said slowly. 'She was killed in the fire.'

A tear ran down Mrs Spinoza's face. 'I'm sorry, Otto,' she said. 'I should have told you about all this long ago but I just didn't know how.' She stood up and walked over to him.

Otto got up too and put his arms around her. 'It doesn't matter, honestly,' he said. 'You brought me up and as far as I'm concerned that makes you my real mother.' For some time they stood there in silence with their arms around each other. Then Otto took a step back. 'Hey! I've just realised something,' he said. 'Strictly speaking I'm older than you. How weird is that!'

Then he laughed. At first Mrs Spinoza looked dismayed but then she too began to laugh. Soon everyone was joining in.

'What are you going to do about the elementarium?' Juliet asked, when the laughter had finally died down.

'I'm going to get rid of it,' Otto replied without hesitation. 'It's nothing but trouble.'

'It's not an easy thing to get rid of,' Mrs Spinoza told him. 'Your stepfather thought he'd done that when he buried it in the garden, but it turned up again.'

'If you'll take my advice, you'll drop it into the middle of Bridlington Loch,' Maximillian said. 'No one will ever find it there. I have a boat moored on the shore and I could take you out in it, if you like.'

'Yes, I think that's a very good idea,' Otto said. 'And the sooner we do it the better.'

'Are you sure that's safe?' Mrs Spinoza asked, her face assuming its habitual anxious frown.

'Don't worry! After what we've been through, I think we can handle a boat trip,' Otto said with a laugh.

'I'll tell you what, I'll go and fetch my car, and we'll go there this evening,' Maximillian said.

When he had left, Otto and Juliet had another chocolate biscuit each. Travelling to other worlds did seem to make you very hungry, Juliet observed.

'There was one more thing I wanted to ask,' Otto said to his mother after a while. 'How did you know to put the clue in your diary?'

'I'd seen the Lily White Boys the week before they kidnapped me,' his mother replied. 'They came into the shop to size it up, I suppose. I didn't like the look of them. They didn't seem to be interested in books, at all. Then after they'd gone I found traces of slime on the bookshelves. So I guessed they were elementals. Your father had warned me about them. He always said they might come looking for you one day.'

Shortly after that, a screech of brakes outside suggested that Maximillian had returned and a moment later the doorbell rang.

'I don't think I'll go with you to the lake, if you don't mind,' Otto's mother said. 'I'm feeling very tired.'

'That's all right, Mum. We won't be long,' Otto replied. He gave her a kiss. Then he, Juliet and Cornelius went downstairs to find Maximillian waiting for them.

Bridlington Loch was a vast grey sheet of water, surrounded by woodland. It was occasionally frequented by fishermen, but on this particular evening there was absolutely no one about. Maximillian parked the car and led them down to a little wooden jetty where a rowing boat was tied up.

Cornelius eyed it with dismay. 'When you said you had a boat, I thought you meant something of a reasonable size,' he complained. 'That thing is no bigger than a matchbox.'

'Don't worry, Corny,' Juliet reassured him. 'There's no need to be scared. I'll hold on to you.'

'Scared!' Cornelius replied indignantly. 'Who says I'm scared? I had just hoped for something a little more dignified, that's all. Cats are not very fond of water, you know.'

Despite Cornelius's reservations, they got into the boat and cast off. Soon Maximillian was rowing them steadily towards the centre of the lake. Out here the lake was very dark and the surface of the water looked like beaten metal.

'I think this will do,' Maximillian said. 'They say that this is one of the deepest lakes in England so I don't think there's much chance of anyone finding it. Are you ready, Otto?'

Otto nodded.

Maximillian rested the oars and the boat glided to a halt. Otto reached into his pocket, took out the elementarium and gazed at it for a moment.

The thought came to him that it might be better to keep it. Perhaps, after all, he might need it one day. You could never tell.

But Otto shook his head. He wasn't fooled. He knew enough to realise that such ideas came from the elementarium itself. They were part of the magic of the thing. It had controlled Belshazzar and Sir Henry, and if he let it, it would control him too.

He took a deep breath, reached out and dropped it overboard.

'Well done, Otto!' Maximillian said. He took up the oars, turned the boat around and headed back to the jetty.

No one spoke much on the way back. Maximillian was preoccupied with rowing, and Juliet, Otto and Cornelius were all busy remembering their adventure. It had suddenly occurred to them that now the elementarium was gone nothing quite so extraordinary was ever likely to happen to them again. A sense of sadness had descended.

When they had got back to the jetty and they were all seated in Maximillian's car, the magical detective paused a moment before turning on the engine.

'There was just one last thing I wanted to ask before we all go our separate ways,' he said.

They others looked at him expectantly.

'What's that?' Otto asked.

'It's just that the Magical Detective Agency has been a bit short-staffed until now. Well, to tell you the truth, there's just been me. And I was wondering whether any of you might be interested in working for me in the future. Of course, the pay's not very good and the conditions can be a bit awful sometimes, and you run the risk of meeting the most terrible people. I suppose nobody in their right mind would want to do the job, really. So I would understand if you all said no, but I just thought I might mention it.' He looked at them hopefully. 'What do you think?'

'Yes!' they all replied simultaneously.

Maximillian grinned from ear to ear. 'Really? Then I think this calls for a celebration. Sherbet lemons all round?'

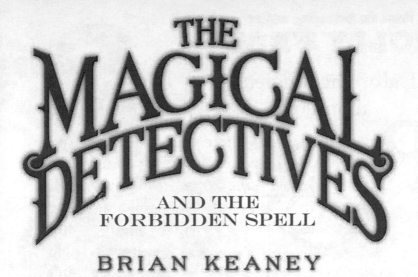

THE MAGICAL DETECTIVES

AND THE FORBIDDEN SPELL

BRIAN KEANEY

Fresh from their weird, wonderful but highly
dangerous adventure in Qullipoth, Otto, Juliet
and Cornelius are now a part of the Magical
Detective Agency — along with the curious,
lemon sherbet-eating Maximilian Hawksmoor.
But they are about to embark on an even riskier
journey to the very heart of magic.
The future is in their hands...

OUT JULY 2011

978 1 40830 682 6 - £5.99 - PB

www.orchardbooks.co.uk
ORCHARD BOOKS

Read on for an extract of
Rose!

ONE

Rose peered out of the corner of the window at the street below, watching interestedly as two little girls walked past with their nursemaid. They were beautifully dressed in matching pale pink coats, and she found them fascinating. How could anyone keep a pink coat clean? She supposed they just weren't allowed to see dirt, ever. The little girls strolled sedately down the street, and Rose stretched up on tiptoe to get one last look as they turned the corner. The bucket she was standing on rocked and clattered alarmingly, and she jumped down in a hurry, hoping no one had heard. The tiny, leaded windows at St Bridget's Home for Abandoned Girls were all very high up, so that the girls were not tempted to look out of them. If any of the matrons realised that Rose had discovered a way to see out, they would do their utmost to stop her, in case her virtue was put at risk by the view of the street. Perhaps they would even outlaw buckets, just in case.

Rose straightened her brown cotton pinafore, and trotted briskly along the deserted passageway to the storeroom to return the bucket. She stowed it carefully on one of the racks of wooden shelves, which was covered in more buckets, brushes and cloths. If anyone saw her, she was planning to say that she had been polishing it.

'Pssst! Rose!' A whisper caught her as she headed for the storeroom door, and Rose shot round, her back against the wall, still nervous.

A small greyish hand beckoned to her from under the bottom shelf, behind a large tin bath. 'Come and see!'

Rose took a deep breath, her heartbeat slowing again. No one had seen her unauthorised use of the bucket. It was only Maisie. 'What are you *doing* under there?' she asked, casting a worried look at the door. 'You'll get in trouble. Come on out.'

'Look,' the whispery voice pleaded, and the greyish fingers dangled something tempting out from under the shelf.

'Oh, Maisie.' Rose sighed. 'I've seen it before, you

know. You showed it to me last week.' But she still crouched down, and wriggled herself under the shelf with her friend.

It was Sunday afternoon. At St Bridget's that meant many of the girls had been in Miss Lockwood's parlour, viewing the Relics. Rose didn't have any Relics, which was why it was a good time for borrowing buckets. Even if anyone saw her, they would probably be too full of silly dreams to care.

'Do you think it's meant to hold a lock of hair?' Maisie asked wistfully. 'Or perhaps a likeness?'

Rose stared thoughtfully at the battered tin locket. It looked as though it had been trodden on, and possibly buried in something nasty, but it was Maisie's most treasured possession – her only possession, for even her clothes were only lent.

'Oh, a likeness, I'm sure,' she told Maisie firmly, wrapping an arm round her friend's bony shoulder. Really she had no idea, but she knew Maisie dreamed about that locket all week, and the hour on Sunday when she got to hold it was her most special time, and Rose couldn't spoil it for her.

'Maybe of my mother. Or perhaps it was hers, and she had my father's picture in it. Yes, that would have been it. I bet he was handsome,' Maisie said dreamily.

'Mmmm,' Rose murmured diplomatically. Maisie

wasn't ugly, exactly, but she was very skinny, and no one looked beautiful with their hair cropped short in case of lice. It was hard to imagine either of her parents as handsome.

All Rose's friends spent Sundays in a dream world, where they were the long-lost daughters of dukes who would one day sweep them away in a coach-and-four to reclaim their rightful inheritance.

Strangely though, unlike all the other girls, Rose did not dream. She had no Relic to hang her dreams on, but that wasn't the main reason. Quite a few of the others didn't either, and it didn't hold them back at all. Rose just wanted to get out of St Bridget's as soon as she possibly could. It wasn't that it was a bad place – the schoolmistress read them lots of improving books about children who weren't lucky enough to have a Home. They lived on the streets, and always went from Bad to Worse in ways that were never very clearly explained. Girls at St Bridget's were fed, even though there was never enough food to actually feel full, only just enough to keep them going. They had clothes, even a set of Sunday best for church, and the yearly photograph. The important thing was, they were trained for domestic service, so that when they were old enough they could earn their own living. If Rose dreamed at all, that was what she dreamed of. She didn't want to be a lady in a big house. She'd settle for being allowed to clean one, and be paid for it. And perhaps have an afternoon off, once a month, although she had no idea what she would do.

Occasionally, girls who'd left St Bridget's came back to show themselves off. They told giggly tales of being admired by the second footman, and they had smart outfits that hadn't been worn by six other girls before them, like Rose's black Sunday dress and coat. She knew because the other girls' names had been sewn in at the top. Two of them even had surnames, which was very grand. Rose was only Rose, and that was because the yellow rose in Miss Lockwood's tiny garden had started to flower on the day she'd been brought to St Bridget's by the vicar. He'd found her in the churchyard, sitting on the war memorial in a fishbasket, and howling. If Rose had been given to dreaming like the others, she might have thought that it meant her father had been a brave soldier, killed in a heroic charge, and that her dying mother couldn't look after her and had left her on the war memorial, hoping that someone would care for a poor soldier's child. As it was, she'd decided her family probably had something to do with fish.

Rose hated fish. Although of course in an orphanage, you ate what there was, and anyone else's if you got half a chance. She knew no grand lady was going to sweep into the orphanage and claim her as a long-lost daughter. It must have been a bad year for fish, that was all. It didn't bother her, and just made her all the more determined to make a life for herself outside.

'What do you think they were like?' Maisie asked pleadingly. Rose was good at storytelling. Somehow her stories lit up the dark corners of the orphanage where they hid to tell them.

Rose sighed. She was tired, but Maisie looked so hopeful. She settled herself as comfortably as she could under the shelf, tucking her dress under her feet to keep warm. The storeroom was damp and chilly, and smelled of wet cleaning cloths. She stared dreamily at the side of the tin bath, glistening in the shadows. 'You were two, weren't you, when you came to St Bridget's?' she murmured. 'So you were old enough to be running about everywhere… Yes. It was a Sunday, and your parents had taken you to the park to sail your boat in the fountain.'

'A boat!' Maisie agreed blissfully.

'Yes, with white sails, and ropes so you could make the sails work, just like real ones.' Rose was remembering the illustrations from *Morally Instructive Tales for the Nursery*, which was one of the books in the schoolroom. The two little boys who owned the boat in the original story fought about who got to sail it first, which obviously meant that one of them drowned in the fountain. Most of the books in the schoolroom had endings like that. Rose quite enjoyed working out the exact point when the characters were beyond hope. It was usually when they'd lied to get more jam.

'You were wearing your best pink coat, but your mother didn't mind if you got it wet.' Rose's voice became rather doubtful here. She hadn't been able to resist putting in the pink coat but really, it was too silly…

Suddenly she realised that Maisie was gazing longingly at the side of the tin bath. 'Yes, look, it's got flower-shaped buttons! Are they roses, Rose?'

Rose gulped. 'I'm not sure,' she murmured, staring wide-eyed at the picture flickering on the metal. 'Daisies, I think…' Had she done that? She knew her stories were good – she was always being bothered for them, so they must be – but none of them had ever come with pictures. Pictures that *moved*. A tiny, plump, pretty Maisie was jumping and clapping as a nattily dressed gentleman blew her boat across a sparkling fountain. *White trousers!* Rose's matter-of-fact side thought disgustedly. *Has this family no sense?*

'Oh, the picture's fading! No, no, bring it back, Rose! I want to see my mother!' Maisie wailed.

'Ssssh! We aren't meant to be here, Maisie, we'll be caught.'

Maisie wasn't listening. 'Oh, Rose, it was so pretty! *I* was so pretty! I want to see it again—'

'Girls!' A sharp voice cut her off. 'What are you doing in here? Come out at once!'

Rose jumped and hit her head on the shelf. The picture promptly disappeared altogether, and Maisie burst into tears.

'Come out of there! Who is that? Rose? And you, Maisie! What on earth are you doing?'

Rose struggled out, trying not to cry herself. Her head really *hurt*, a horrible sharp throbbing that made her feel sick. Of all the stupid things to do! This was what happened when you started making pictures on baths. Miss Lockwood looked irritable. 'Maisie, you know you're not supposed to take that out of my office,' she snapped, reaching down and seizing the locket. The flimsy chain broke, and Maisie howled even louder, tugging at the trailing end.

Rose could tell that Miss Lockwood was horrified. She really hadn't meant to snap the locket, and she knew how Maisie treasured it. But she couldn't draw back now. 'Silly girl! Now you've broken it. Well, it's just what you deserve.' Red in the face, she stuffed it into the little hanging pocket she wore on her belt, and swept out. 'Go to bed at once! There will be no supper for either of you!' she announced grandly at the door.

'Well, that's no great loss,' Rose muttered, putting an arm round Maisie, who was crying in great heaving gulps.

'She – broke – my – locket!'

'Yes,' Rose admitted gently. 'Yes, she did. But I'm sure we can mend it. Next Sunday. I'll help, Maisie, I promise. And I don't think she meant to. I think she was sorry, Maisie. She could have made us stand in the schoolroom with books on our heads all evening, like she did to Florence last week. No supper's not that bad. It would only be bread and milk.'

'It might not be,' sniffed Maisie, who seemed determined to look on the black side of things. 'It might be cake.'

Rose took her hand as they trailed dismally back to their dormitory. 'Maisie, it's *always* bread and milk! The last time we had cake was for the coronation, nearly three years ago!' Rose sighed. She couldn't help feeling cross with Maisie for getting her into trouble, but not *very* cross. After all, she'd been tempting fate with the windows anyway. Maisie was so tiny and fragile that Rose always felt sorry for her. 'Do you want me to tell you a story?' she asked resignedly, as they changed into their nightclothes.

'Will you make the pictures come again?' Maisie asked, her eyes lighting up.

'I don't know,' Rose told her honestly. 'It's never happened before. And there might be trouble if we get caught, I'm sure it's not allowed.'

'It isn't in the Rules,' Maisie said, pouting. 'I know it isn't.'

Miss Lockwood read the Rules on Sundays before church, so they'd heard them that morning. Rose had to admit that Maisie was right, she didn't remember a rule about making pictures on baths. Which was odd – it must mean that it wasn't a very common thing to do, because the Rules covered *everything*. Even the exact length of an orphan's fingernails.

'It just feels like something that wouldn't be allowed…' Rose said. *Which is why it's such fun*, part of her wanted to add. 'Oh, all right. But I think it needs something shiny for it to work.' She looked round thoughtfully. The dormitory was long and narrow, high up in the attics of the old house. Everything was very clean, but shiny was in short supply. There was hardly room for the girls to move between the narrow, grey-blanketed beds, let alone space for polished furniture.

Maisie followed her, craning her neck to peer into corners. 'My boots are shiny!' she suggested brightly.

Rose was about to say they couldn't be, then realised that Maisie was right. All the girls' shoes were made and mended by the boys from St Bartholomew's orphanage over the wall. They had a cobblers' workshop where the girls had a laundry, so that they could be trained up for a useful trade. Maisie's boots had just come back from being mended, and they were black and shiny, even if they'd been patched so often that there was nothing left of the original boot. If she could make pictures on a bath, why not a boot?

The two girls sat huddled together under Rose's blankets, staring at the polished leather. 'It'll be a lot smaller, if it even works,' Rose warned.

'I don't mind.' Maisie didn't take her eyes off the boot. 'I want to see what happened.'

'It isn't really what happened…' Rose reminded her. 'Just a story I'm making up, you know that, don't you?'

'Yes, yes.' Maisie flapped her hand at Rose irritably, but Rose didn't think she was really listening. 'Show me!'

Long after Maisie had cried herself to sleep that night – heartbroken by the flickering image of her tiny self running through the park and crying for her mother – and the other girls had come chattering to bed, Rose lay awake.

Had she made it all up? It had seemed so real, somehow. *What if I've turned into a fortune-teller?* Rose worried to herself. She didn't *believe* in fortune-tellers. But of course she'd invented it – she'd put in that pink coat, from the little girls she'd seen out of the window. So if it wasn't real, why had it upset Maisie so much? Why had she believed it more than all Rose's other stories? *The pictures*, Rose told herself. *The pictures made it seem too real. I wanted to believe it, too. I'm not doing that again.*

Next to her, Maisie's breath was still catching as she slept, her thin shoulders shuddering, as if she were dreaming it all over again, the lost child that she believed was her, running round the glittering fountain to fetch her boat, then turning back and seeing only other children's parents.

Rose didn't know how she'd done it. This had never happened when she told stories before today. She hadn't done anything differently, not that she could think of. But she must never, ever let it happen again. It was too strong. Rose was sure she'd made it up – or almost sure – but now Maisie had seen it, for her it was real. She would remember it for ever.

Although, Rose thought, as she eventually closed her eyes, *if it were true, the boat would be in Miss Lockwood's office, with the other Relics…* So it couldn't be. It was just a story. But her stories had never frightened her before.